INSPECTOR PAWS
AND THE ALASKAN ICE CAP

ROSEMARY BUDD

INSPECTOR PAWS AND THE ALASKAN ICE CAP

iUniverse books may be ordered through booksellers or by contacting:

iUniverse
1663 Liberty Drive
Bloomington, IN 47403
www.iuniverse.com
1-800-Authors (1-800-288-4677)

Because of the dynamic nature of the Internet, any web addresses or links contained in this book may have changed since publication and may no longer be valid. The views expressed in this work are solely those of the author and do not necessarily reflect the views of the publisher, and the publisher hereby disclaims any responsibility for them.

Any people depicted in stock imagery provided by Thinkstock are models, and such images are being used for illustrative purposes only. Certain stock imagery © Thinkstock.

ISBN: 978-1-4917-8096-1 (sc)
ISBN: 978-1-4917-8098-5 (hc)
ISBN: 978-1-4917-8097-8 (e)

Library of Congress Control Number: 2015918630

Print information available on the last page.

iUniverse rev. date: 11/5/2015

To Carol, Doreen, Helen, Renee, Ellen and Evie, my wonderful Alaskan cruising companions.

CHAPTER 1

"A CAT!"

The woman's shriek sent me scurrying for cover. I'd run into her sort before in my old alley-cat days. She was the kind who threw a bucket over your head if you so much as sniffed at her garden and then called the animal control people to put you out of your misery.

I scooted under the nearest deckchair, slithered beneath an abandoned straw sunhat, and peered out at the woman.

If this cruise ship was called *The Spirit of the North*, then the woman dressed totally in black — black sandals, black cropped pants, black tee shirt with absolutely no bling, black sun glasses, and black sun visor — must be the siren of doom assigned to toss unsuspecting souls overboard as fodder for Davey Jones' locker. Her only splash of color — a bright red slash across her face where her lips pressed firmly together — did nothing to ease my trembling whiskers. She shifted tote bags, cushions, and deckchairs, obviously hunting for me. I held my breath and checked to make sure my tail was firmly tucked under the hat. That appendage had a bad habit of giving away my whereabouts.

Her black sandals slipped under my deckchair. She lifted a tote bag off the chair, put it back down, shuffled a newspaper. The toe of her sandal bumped into the sunhat. My body tensed, ready to flee. Her sandal quickly withdrew as a man approached.

The man was dressed totally in white, from his white loafers to the thick wavy locks of hair that peeked out from under his white cap. He had the firm square jaw of a man used to giving orders. Must be one of the crew members. A whole pack of similar white uniforms had chased after me as I raced up nine flights of stairs and dashed around nine huge decks in my search for Stella and Max.

Stella called herself my caretaker, but great balls of fur, she was the one that needed to be taken care of. She'd come on this ship knowing full well she was headed for danger. And if that wasn't bad enough, she'd dragged her granddaughter, Max, along with her. I needed to find them and get them off this ship before it sailed, but how was I going to do that tucked under this straw bonnet?

"What kind of ship are you running, Gideon?" the lady demanded. She seemed to have almost as much derision for the man as she did for me. "I just saw a cat."

The man ignored her comment.

"Bon Voyage, Sis," he said. The smile that slid across his face with the ease of a well-worn sweater, softening the firmness of his jaw and crinkling the weathered skin around his eyes, proved he was a man used to dealing with difficult people. He handed the siren of doom a tall yellow glass topped with a slice of orange and a tiny pink umbrella. "Here's your complimentary drink, Sis! Raise your glass to a delightful cruise."

Free drinks? I breathed a sigh of relief and relaxed under my sunhat. If they were handing out free drinks — especially fancy drinks with pink umbrellas — Stella would be here sooner or later. I hoped it was sooner.

"I tell you, Gideon, I saw a cat," the woman said. She pulled a sani-wipe from her handbag, wiped off the rim of her glass, and held her drink at arm's length.

Was she afraid the color might contaminate her black outfit? And I thought Stella and her zany friend Jo were weird. Humans! They're beyond comprehension.

"Nonsense!" The man took a sip of his drink. "What would a cat be doing aboard a cruise ship?"

"That's what I want to know," the lady demanded. "This is your ship, Gideon. I hope you're still striving for excellence, not slacking off, letting the crew get away with who knows what."

The man's comfortable smile slipped a little, and his jaw tightened. "Let's get one thing straight, Miriam," he said. "I'm not your little brother now in need of mothering and advice. I'm a grown man, captain of this ship."

Captain? A tremor of fear set my whiskers tingling again. If he was the captain, what was he doing here downing drinks and chit-chatting with passengers? Shouldn't he be in the wheel house or wherever it is they steer the ship from?

"If you want to do some mothering, Miriam," the captain continued, "you can keep an eye on Alvin for me."

Miriam heaved a sigh that set the paper umbrella on her drink flapping.

"As to Alvin," she started, but whatever she was going to say about Alvin remained unsaid. Her eyes widened. She grabbed the captain's arm and waved her drink in the direction of the doorway.

"That's Leroy Garvey," she said accusingly.

I poked my head out from under the hat. Leroy Garvey? The man Stella's friend Jo was about to marry? The one who'd threatened Stella? Stella had called Jo this morning, but Leroy Garvey took the call and refused to let her talk to Jo. "I don't want to see you on that cruise," he'd said. I could hear the threat in his voice even from my perch on Stella's lap. "Accidents can happen at sea, you know," he said.

I slid further out from under the hat for a better look. He was shorter than I'd expected. The top of his head only reached as high as Jo's shoulder. He wore a white suit to rival the captain's, but his paunch had popped open the buttons at the bottom. The navy blue scarf tucked into the open neck of his jacket reflected the steely blue of his eyes, a blue as dark and cold as the churning waves behind him. He smiled up at Jo. Jo, dressed in a matching sailor suit, smiled back at him.

Great furry hairballs! Where was Stella? I needed to find her and get her off this ship before she ran into Leroy Garvey. I jumped onto the railing and scanned the deck.

"Why didn't you tell me Leroy Garvey would be on this cruise?" Miriam snapped.

The captain ignored her question, but his strong sinewy hand slid under my midsection and lifted me high above the railing. I tried to yowl for help, but the cry froze in my throat. I gazed in terror as the steely blue waves below me slurped and slapped at the sides of the boat. If there's anything I hate, it's falling. You can forget that flea-brained theory that cats always land on their feet. I know from experience it's not true. Just the thought of falling into that sea full of churning waves turned me into a shuddering ball of fear.

"Would you look at this, Miriam," the captain said, his smile widening until his whole face was crinkled with laughter lines. "I've caught our little stowaway. A stowaway cat. Now that's a first."

His eyes, the same blue as the slurping, slapping waves, sparkled with devilish glee as he stared into my terrified ones.

"Now where did you come from?" he asked.

"Never mind the cat." Miriam plopped her drink on the arm of a deck chair and reached for a black sweater slung over the back. "Help me get off this ship. I'm not sailing with Leroy Garvey."

The captain frowned. "For goodness sakes, Miriam," he said. "That was ages ago. I thought you'd be over it by now. Anyway, it's a big ship."

"No ship is big enough to share with that man," Miriam snapped. "I'm getting off."

A blast louder than any fog horn I'd ever heard rent the air. I'd have jumped overboard, waves or no waves, if the captain's hand hadn't tightened around me. He drew me close to his chest. I tried to resist, but the ship's horn gave another blast every bit as loud as the last one. I burrowed my head into his shoulder trying to block out the noise.

"Too late to get off now," the captain said when the sound of the whistle died away. "This boat's underway."

Underway? I could feel the motion even as the captain said it. The ship indeed was moving. But this was the captain's shoulder my head was burrowed into. So who was driving this thing?

I lifted my head and yowled in terror.

CHAPTER 2

THE SHIP'S WHISTLE HAD raised the noise level of the chattering passengers to even more deafening heights. A trio of giggling teenage girls leaned precariously over the railing beside us, waving madly to their friends on shore. A balding man with a voice even louder than his shirt waved a camera over his head and bellowed for his wife and daughters to get over here and get their picture taken. A pair of white-haired couples long past their best before dates clung to their walkers with one hand, raised their tall yellow glasses in the other, and belted out the chorus of *North to Alaska,* which wouldn't have been half so bad if any of them could carry a tune.

My terrified yowl brought them all to a frozen standstill. Every eye turned to stare at me. I struggled to escape the captain's embrace, but his giant paw tightened around me like a vise.

"Inspector Paws!" a woman shrieked.

That was Stella's shriek. I could see her bleached blonde curls bouncing as she barreled her way through the crowd. Her spiky red stilettos beating time to their own tune, she parted the colorful array of bodies as though she were Moses parting the Red Sea.

I could tell from her use of my full name that I was in trouble. It didn't matter that it was hardly my fault I was on this ship. I'd still get blamed for it. Stella only called me by my full name when I'd done something that annoyed her. Her late husband, Ernie, named me shortly after I'd decided to give up my alley-cat days and bunk in the relative safety of the Clayton home. He found me hiding under the couch one day. I was perched on an Inspector Morse novel at the time and reluctant to let go of it. "So you like detective stories, do you?" Ernie said. "What a clever cat." Ernie was a man of rare judgment. After that he called me Inspector Paws. Stella said it was too long and cumbersome. She shortened it to Paws — except when I broke one of her endless list of idiotic rules.

"Inspector Paws!" Stella shrieked again. "What are you doing here?"

Stella's shriek released the crowd from their frozen trance. Fingers pointed at me. The trio of teenage girls giggled and gushed. The creaky quartet screamed as though I were some monster who'd leaped at them from the bottom of the sea. Stella shoved past them and stared up at me, her mouth wide open and her brown eyes nearly bulging out of her head.

I clawed at the captain's shoulder in an even more desperate attempt to escape. All that did was dislodge one of the shiny brass buttons. It plopped into the top of Stella's tall yellow glass. Bright pink liquid splattered into my face and onto the sleeve of the captain's white jacket.

If Stella had a drink in her hand, that meant she'd been here for a while. Why hadn't I seen her earlier? I yowled at her, trying to warn her that we needed to get off this boat, but her gaze skimmed past me and fixed onto the strip of decoration adorning the shoulder of the captain's jacket, now missing one of its brass buttons. Her eyes widened even more, although I hadn't thought that possible.

"Captain?" Her voice was tentative and had more than a question in it.

The captain's easy smile slid across his face, and his eyes lit up with a look that made me even more uneasy. Ignoring the bright pink stain on his sleeve, the captain held out a hand to Stella. "Captain Bonar, at your service, Ma'am," he said. "I presume this little stowaway belongs to you."

Stella's free hand went to her mouth. "Oh, Captain, I'm so sorry," she apologized.

Sorry? Great balls of fur! This was no time for apologies. I yowled at her again. We had to find Max and jump ship now before it was too late.

I glanced over her shoulder and knew it was already too late. The giant sails of the cruise ship terminal shrank smaller and smaller into the distance. Safe harbor was behind us. I glanced towards the doorway. And danger was rushing straight at us.

Jo, Stella's best friend, the one Ernie called Crazy Jo, the one who wore costumes everyday as though she were in some sort of perpetual stage play, the one who invariably got Stella into even more trouble than she would have all by herself, was headed straight for us. As if that weren't enough, she had a hand clamped firmly around the arm of Leroy Garvey and was dragging him along with her.

I reached for Stella, but my claws only caught the edge of her yellow glass. The glass tumbled from her hand. Bright pink liquid poured down the captain's white pant leg.

"Stella!" Jo's excited voice rose above the din. Her sailor's hat flew off as she let go of Leroy's arm and raced over to us. She hugged Stella as though they'd been separated for years. Wasn't it just yesterday they'd been sitting at the counter in Stella's kitchen arguing about Jo's hasty marriage to the mysterious, and according to Stella's son, ruthless Leroy Garvey?

"I'm so glad you're here." Jo hugged Stella again. "Leroy said that something came up and you weren't coming."

"Did he?" Stella looked coldly at Leroy. "I think Leroy misunderstood me. Or perhaps he underestimated my resourcefulness."

Leroy acknowledged Stella with a slight nod of the head. The blood vessels on his forehead bulged. He slid his sun glasses off and gave Stella a flitting smile that barely reached his face let alone his eyes.

"My mistake, Stella," he said. "It won't happen again." He tapped his sunglasses against the cold, flashy diamond of the ring encircling the middle finger of his right hand. His voice grew quieter. "I do hope you won't underestimate me."

A tremor of fear raced up my spine. That was a threat if I ever heard one. I hissed a warning. Garvey's eyes widened, and he jumped back as though I'd slashed his face with my claws. I sank back into the captain's arms in amazement. Leroy Garvey was afraid of me. Perhaps he wasn't such a threat after all. How terrifying can anyone be who's afraid of a little pussy cat?

Garvey continued to back into the crowd. It was only when he was a good ten feet away that he pulled himself back up to his full height, stood on his tiptoes, and peered over the shoulder of the startled woman in front of him. The blood vessels on his forehead still bulging, he glared straight at the captain.

"I'm going for one of those drinks you're wearing, Captain Bonar," he called. "And when I get back I expect that cat to be gone." The unspoken "or else" hung in the air between them.

"Oh, Stella, how could you?" Jo asked. She looked worriedly at Leroy as though trying to decide if she should chase after him, but instead she turned back to Stella with a frown. "Why on earth would you bring Inspector Paws? Surely you know cats aren't allowed on cruise ships."

"I didn't bring him," Stella protested.

"I brought him, Aunt Jo," Max's unmistakable voice piped up.

But where was it coming from? I peered over the captain's shoulder. Max's freckled face and bright red hair, followed by her bouncing ponytail, poked its way between two of the aged choristers. She edged her way between them and squeezed past the metal barrier created by their walkers as they gazed up at us unashamedly eavesdropping. Their mouths gaped so wide it was a wonder their teeth hadn't fallen out.

Max was Stella in miniature, although at thirteen, there was no longer anything miniature about her. Only last week she'd stood back-to-back with Stella, gloating that she'd now caught up to her in height. They didn't look alike. Max had the lean, willowy frame of an athletic teenager. Stella had the well-padded frame of someone who'd enjoyed gourmet meals and chocolate truffles for more years than she cared to disclose. But in the things that count, they were exactly alike. Far too curious for their own good. Nosey was the word Ernie used. "Mark my words," Ernie would say to Stella. "That nose of yours is going to get you in trouble one of these days." Not that that every stopped her. And both Stella and Max were far too reckless. Rushing into things without giving any thought to how they were going to get themselves out. Seemed to think rules — even the rules of nature — couldn't possibly apply to them.

"You brought Paws?" Stella's mouth gaped almost as wide as those of the gaping eavesdroppers.

"Of course, Gran," Max said. Her ponytail flicked back and forth slapping the eavesdropper behind her. His glasses slid down his well-wrinkled face and balanced crookedly on the end of his nose.

"Seriously, Gran," Max continued. "You didn't think I'd

leave him there all alone with that mean old Mrs. McKeever, did you?"

Mrs. McKeever, Stella's cranky housekeeper, had absolutely no love for cats, especially me. "Cat hair everywhere," she grumbled. "And fur balls under every piece of furniture. Why they keep you around is beyond me." And then she'd chase me around the room with that noisy, vibrating vacuum cleaner. I couldn't count the number of times my tail had come near to being sucked into the belly of that beast.

"But how did you get him on board?" Stella asked, her mouth still gaping.

"I hid him in one of your shoe bags," Max replied.

And if you think a vacuum cleaner can put a kink in your tail, try bouncing around in the trunk of a car stashed in a bag full of high-heeled shoes. Just the memory of it brought the pain back to my bruised appendage. I licked at it furiously. It was a small price to pay, though, for the chance to escape being left alone with the sadistic Mrs. McKeever. And besides, I had to stop Max and Stella from getting on that ship somehow, didn't I? Hadn't I promised Ernie that I'd keep them out of trouble?

"Keep an eye on Stella for me, Inspector Paws," he'd said as he patted my head and left for work the day he never returned. "Don't let her get in any trouble."

How was I supposed to keep an eye on Stella stuck at home with the cranky Mrs. McKeever?

"I'm afraid I had to leave your candy-striped sneakers and your orange stilettos at home to make room for him, Gran," Max said. She gave Stella her sheepish look of apology that could melt the most hardened of hearts. "Hope you won't miss them."

With two travel cases full of shoes for a seven day cruise, it was hardly likely Stella would miss two pairs, no matter how colorful.

"Really, Max. What were you thinking?" Jo said. She looked nervously over to the bar where Leroy was loudly demanding his complementary drinks. "Even you should have known cats aren't allowed on cruise ships."

"But Aunt Jo." Max turned her pleading eyes to Jo. "We couldn't possibly do an investigation without Inspector Paws."

"An investigation?" Jo's eyes darted from Max to Stella and back again. "What investigation?"

"Leroy Garvey, of course," Max said. Her ponytail flicked back and forth, once more knocking the eavesdropper's glasses askew. "We're going to find out everything we can about him. We can't let you marry someone you don't know anything about. Isn't that right, Gran?" She turned to Stella, who was flapping her hands like a wild bird trying to shush her.

"Oh, Stella!" Jo cried. Her face crumpled into that look she always got just before she burst into tears. "I do wish you'd try to get to know Leroy better. He's not at all as bad as you think. You'll love him once you get to know him. Don't you agree, Captain Bonar?"

She turned to the captain for back up, but Captain Bonar didn't reply. He stood as though frozen to the spot. His startled eyes stared at Max. His mouth gaped wider than any aging eavesdropper's could ever hope to gape.

I realized now that his grip on me had loosened. I could easily escape. But curiosity, the bane of all cats and the trait I'd just accused Stella and Max of having too much of, held me firmly in place.

What could there possibly be about Max that had this strong, confident Captain of the *Spirit of the North* staring at her like she'd just sprouted two heads?

⟨ CHAPTER 3

I DIDN'T HAVE TO wait long for the answer.

A rollicking laugh rose above the crowd's noisy chatter and drew my attention to the doorway. The rippling waves of merriment came from a short, stocky man with the build of a wrestler and the face of a joyful cherub. He wore the white uniform of a crew member, but it fitted rather tightly on his large frame. The brass buttons strained to keep the white jacket from gaping open. His head, which had been shaved completely bald, appeared almost too big for his body, and with each roiling burst of laughter, it shook like a bobble-head. The large double hoops of gold dangling from one of his ears jangled like a pair of cymbals.

He wended his way through the crowd of passengers, greeting each one with his boisterous laugh and a hearty slap on the back that had them tilting every which way. But it was the person he was dragging along behind him that made me sit up and take a second, and then a third, and then a fourth look.

I hadn't been sipping any of those fancy drinks with the pink umbrellas, but I was definitely seeing double. There were two Maxes. One stood right beside me, her long, red ponytail swinging back and forth in disbelief, and the other, dressed in the white uniform of a crew member, the red hair tucked into a clashing red baseball cap, was being dragged reluctantly toward us by the jolly cherub.

"Ahoy there, Captain," the cherub called as he got nearer. "I've found the solution, sir." He laughed loudly. His head bobbled. The gold hoops jangled. He tugged on the arm of his reluctant Max and propelled them both forward until they stood right in front of the captain.

Captain Bonar woke from his trance. His grip on me tightened.

"Akito," he said

Whatever else he was about to say was interrupted by Max's piping voice.

"OMG!" she shrieked. "I could be looking in a mirror." She shoved her way past the captain and stared up into the equally startled eyes of her look-alike. "Except you're a little taller than me," she added.

There was another difference between Max and her look-alike. He was a boy.

"Who are you?" Max asked.

The boy didn't answer.

The jolly cherub's head bobbled back and forth, back and forth, looking from one to the other. "Oh my! Oh, my!" he repeated with each bobble. He laughed, and his gold earring jangled again. "You didn't tell me you had a sister, Alvin," he said.

"He doesn't," the captain snapped. His voice was clipped, his jaw tight.

The cherub's eyebrows lifted questioningly.

As though realizing he had sounded a little harsh, the captain forcibly softened his voice.

"It's obviously just a coincidence," he said.

He didn't sound entirely convinced.

"They say everyone has a look-alike somewhere," the captain continued. "It's just not often one gets to meet there's, is it?" He put a hand on Max's shoulder. "Max Clayton, let me introduce to you to your look-alike." He paused. His hand slipped off Max's shoulder, and clamped onto the boy's. He drew the boy closer. "My son, Alvin," he said. "Who's working for the summer as a room steward," he added.

So this was Alvin, the one the captain had asked his sister to keep an eye on. If Alvin was anything like Max, it's no wonder the captain was worried about him. But Alvin didn't appear to be at all like Max, except in looks. Max shrieked excitedly and bounced from foot to foot, while Alvin yanked free of his father's touch, tugged on the brim of his baseball cap to further hide his eyes, and withdrew into sullen silence.

"But they're so much alike," Jo said. "Surely they must be related."

The captain ignored her comment, but his jaw tightened.

And this," the captain continued as though Jo hadn't spoken. "This is your cruise director, Lorne Akito." He drew the smiling cherub forward.

The cherub shook Stella's hand and then clasped Jo's in both of his.

"Oh my! Oh my! It's the bride-to-be!" he said. He laughed loudly. His head bobbled. His earring jangled. "I'm so, so excited. A wedding cruise. There's just nothing better. And to think you picked us for your special event. I promise you won't regret it!"

I couldn't help the growl that rumbled inside me and burst out in a loud, angry hiss. Regret it? Of course Jo would regret it. She was about to make the biggest mistake of her life marrying that thug Leroy Garvey.

Captain Bonar squished me against his chest so I could barely breath, let alone express any further opinion.

"What was it you wanted to see me about, Akito?" the captain asked. "You said something about finding a solution. A solution to what?"

"Oh my!" Akito said. He let go of Jo's hand and turned back to the captain. He laughed loudly. His head bobbled. His earring jangled. "I almost forgot. The guitar player didn't show." He turned apologetically towards Stella and Jo. "My first chance as a cruise director, and I wanted everything to be so perfect," he said. "Wouldn't you know it? The guitar player misses the boat." He laughed again. His head bobbled. His earring jangled. "Anyway," he said, turning back to the captain. "I found the solution."

I could feel the captain's grip on me tighten even more. He looked from Akito to Alvin and back again.

Lorne Akito put a hand on Alvin's shoulder and pulled him forward. "Your son, Alvin, is the best guitar player I've ever heard, sir. He could ..."

"Absolutely not!" the captain barked, not letting Akito finish his sentence. He glared at Alvin. "Didn't I tell you there was to be no music this summer?"

Alvin pulled the ball cap further down on his head, shrugged off Lorne's hand, and turned toward the door. "Told you he wouldn't listen," he muttered.

"But, sir ..." Lorne attempted another plea, but the captain cut him short.

"The answer is no, and if you treasure your job, Akito, you won't encourage the boy."

"Come on, Lorne," Alvin muttered. He stomped toward the door. "There's no point. Once the old man's made up his mind, there's no changing it."

The captain drew in a deep breath.

"The old man is captain to you for the duration of this cruise, son," he said. His voice had gone soft and quiet, and was almost as threatening as Leroy Garvey's had been. "And I told you to get rid of that cap."

Alvin spun in the doorway, doffed his cap, and gave the captain a mock salute. "Aye, aye, Captain!" he said. He plopped the cap back on his head, turned on his heel, and sped out the door.

Lorne gave the captain another startled look, and then scurried after Alvin.

Captain Bonar sighed. His grip on me slackened a little, enough so I could breathe again. He rubbed his forehead as though trying to force the frown lines away.

"My apologies, ladies," he said to Stella and Jo. "You're so lucky not to have to raise a teenage son," he said.

"Oh, I've been there, done that," Stella said.

She was referring to Max's father, Stewart, of course, but I had trouble picturing Stewart as a teenager. He'd been old and bossy ever since I knew him. Always ordering Stella about, not that it did him much good.

Stella laid a comforting hand on the captain's arm. The captain's face brightened, and he looked warmly down at Stella.

I didn't like that look. There was something about it that sent an uneasy tingling through every one of my whiskers.

"Wait!" Max called out.

Her shriek made us all jump.

"I've got an idea!" she yelled.

She raced after Alvin and Lorne, her red ponytail bouncing up and down like a flag of danger.

Great balls of fur! Max with an idea was like a lighted match next to a gasoline tank. Somebody had to stop her. I struggled to free myself from the captain's clutches, but his grip tightened. Once more I couldn't breathe. I let out a strangled squawk. It wasn't much of a squawk, but enough to get Stella's attention.

"Oh, Captain, you're squishing Paws," she objected. "Maybe I should hold him."

She reached for me, but the captain pulled me away.

"Oh, no, Ma'am," he said. He gave Stella that look again. Another uneasy tremor raced through my whiskers. "Or may I call you Stella?" he asked.

His smile was that of a tom who's caught scent of an attractive feline of the female variety. Great balls of fur! No wonder my whiskers were tingling uneasily. Didn't I have enough to worry about without this prowling tom setting his sights on Stella?

I let out another strangled yowl.

The captain's grip on me loosened a little. I gulped in a lungful of air.

"I'm afraid this little stowaway is headed for the brig," he said. He smiled apologetically at Stella.

The brig? Wasn't that what they called the ship's jail? How would I look out for Stella and Max if I were stuck in the brig?

I dug my back feet into the captain's chest and thrust myself forward. The captain swore under his breath as my claws dug into his flesh. His hand sprang open, and I flew through the air.

I hadn't noticed Leroy Garvey returning. He held a colorful glass in each hand, his head turned toward Jo as he called something over his shoulder.

Was it my fault that he walked right in front of me?

I smacked into his head. My claws dug into his white captain's hat as I struggled to keep my balance. The drinks flew out of his hand. Bright, pink liquid splashed down the front of his white jacket.

I didn't wait around for his bellow, but leaped to the floor and raced wildly out the door where Max had disappeared. Leroy's threatening voice chased me down the corridor and sent chills up my spine as I skidded around the corner.

"Throw that cat overboard, Captain," Garvey yelled. "Or I'll do it for you!"

CHAPTER 4

I SKIDDED TO A stop at the door to the Sea Nymphs Cafeteria. The mixture of tantalizing aromas drew me inside. There was no sign of Max amongst the colorful array of passengers chattering like magpies and shoving food into their mouths, but the smell of freshly grilled salmon set my taste buds on high alert. My mouth watered in anticipation. Several sizzling, golden chickens turned temptingly on a spit. Even the slabs of roast beef looked like they'd melt in my mouth given half the chance. I looked longingly at the abundant display of my favorite foods, but there wasn't time to indulge. I needed to find Max.

Snitching a pawful of salmon from the nearest platter, I scurried out the door and nearly fell into another swimming pool.

A second swimming pool? Why'd they need two? There was already far too much water sloshing back and forth around the outside of this boat. Why did they want more water inside the boat? Humans! There was just no understanding them.

I skittered under the nearest deck chair and tried to quell my churning stomach, only to come eye-to-eye with one of the more colorful representatives of the human species. She was sprawled on the deck chair next to mine sipping one of those fancy drinks in the tall yellow glass with the pink umbrella. A mass of bleached yellow curls poked disobediently out from under the neon green sunhat that tilted lopsidedly over her face. Excess folds of skin bulged out of her skimpy orange swimsuit, their rosy hue indicating they'd been in the sun longer than was healthy. The matching rosy glow on her half-hidden face told me she'd not only had more sun than she needed, but more of those fancy drinks. She gave me a crooked smile and lifted her glass in salute.

"Long live the cat!" she yelled. Her slurred yell was loud enough to wake the dead. Startled sunbathers toppled off their deck chairs and turned to stare at us. A man on the diving board slipped off and did a belly flop in the pool. Two white uniforms raced toward us.

Great balls of fur! I had to get out of here before they threw me in the brig.

I darted out from under the deck chair, leaped over the drunken sun worshiper, and fled out of the pool area. Skidding around the corner, I ducked into the nearest room. I closed my eyes, and held my breath as the cursing crew members clattered past. It wasn't until the sounds of my pursuers faded down the hallway that I dared open my eyes and look around the room I'd landed in.

It was a small room, almost dark compared to the sun-drenched pool area. Soft guitar music — the kind Ernie used to listen to — floated through the air, filling me with a longing for Ernie. Ernie had been the very best of the human species, my protector, my confidante, the only one who'd truly understood me. I wished I could right now curl up in his well-worn armchair, feel his hand caress my fur, and let the music wrap me in a soft cocoon.

A strange crooning sound startled me out of my reverie. My eyes widened in dismay. Not two paws in front of me, squatted in a lotus position, her dark attire blending into the shadows of the room, sat the captain's sister, Miriam, the siren of doom.

"Ohmmm ... Ohmmm," she hummed.

Great balls of fur! The siren's song. She'd lured me in here with her siren's song, and as soon as she opened her eyes, she'd nab me and toss me into the sea as fodder for Davey Jones' locker.

I started to sidle backwards out of the room, but the doorway was blocked by a teenage girl. I darted under a nearby bench, squeezed as far into the shadows as possible, and peered out at the girl.

She appeared to be a few years older than Max, perhaps in her late teens. Teetering in the doorway on spiky-heeled sandals, with her porcelain skin, baby blue eyes, and hair the color of the mid-day sun, she looked more like a fairy princess than a teenage girl.

Should I warn her that she was about to step into the siren's den?

I opened my mouth to yowl a warning, but quickly closed it again. It was too late. The princess gazed at Miriam with such adoration, it was clear she'd already fallen under the siren's spell.

"Mrs. Turner," she whispered in a tone of awe, as though the Great Creator himself had fallen under her gaze.

The siren didn't even open her eyes, just continued her monotonous chant.

"Ohmmm ... Ohmmm."

The princess took a tentative step into the room, and then, as though she couldn't help herself, she rushed all the way in.

"I'm so sorry to disturb you, Mrs. Turner," she gushed. "But I'm such a big fan of yours. I've read every one of your books." She hurriedly dug into the voluminous tote slung over her shoulder, and pulled out a book. "I found this one in the gift shop and ... really ... I just ... would you sign it?"

Miriam Turner's droning came to an abrupt stop. Her eyes flicked opened. She looked up at the girl, a smile softening the harsh edges of her face.

Great balls of fur! The siren could smile. Or was that part of the spell?

Miriam reached out a hand to the girl. "Oh, do come in," she said. "Your words have brought me more relief than a whole half-hour of meditation."

She took the book from the girl's outstretched hand. Pulling a package of sani-wipes from her nearby purse, she wiped the jacket of the book thoroughly. She did the same to the pen the girl handed her, and then opened the book.

"Who shall I make this out to?" Miriam asked, her pen poised above the fly leaf.

"Patricia Garvey," the girl said.

Miriam Turner's hand froze above the page. She looked at the girl, her smile evaporating as quickly as it had appeared.

"Leroy Garvey's daughter?" she snapped.

"Why yes." The girl looked at her in delight. "Do you know him?"

Miriam Turner didn't reply.

The girl's face crumpled into a look of dismay. "Oh," she said. "You've had a run-in with Daddy, haven't you? He's not a big fan of your books. Says they fill my head with nonsense."

Miriam raised her eyebrows.

"But he's not a woman, is he?" Patricia continued. She tossed her blond hair over her shoulder with a defiant flip of her head. "And he's just a bit old fashioned, you know. He doesn't like it that you teach us girls to think for ourselves, to set goals, to make our dreams come true."

Miriam looked at her thoughtfully. Her smile slid slowly back into place. She signed the book with a flourish.

"And what are your dreams, Patricia?" Miriam asked as she handed the book back.

Patricia's face came alive with joy. Her baby blue eyes sparkled as though someone had turned on the lights inside her. She grasped the book tightly to her chest and looked up at the ceiling.

"Oh, Mrs. Turner!" she said. "I have such dreams. Someday ..." Her voice lowered to almost a whisper and she gave Miriam Turner a look of conspiracy. "Someday I'm going to run Daddy's company."

Miriam Turner's black-painted eyebrows arched even higher.

"I can do it. I know I can," Patricia said. "Daddy says I can't. He says it takes a man to run a business as complicated as his. He wants me to marry that stuffy Angus Lloyd, his right-hand man, and let Angus run the company, but I have other ideas."

Ideas? Great furry hairballs! How'd I gotten so easily distracted? Max was somewhere on this boat with one of her flea-brained ideas. I had to find her. I had to stop her. I darted out of my hiding place and rushed past the startled fairy princess.

"The cat!" Miriam's shriek echoed behind me as I raced down the corridor and out of her sight.

As I padded cautiously around the corner beside the stairwell, I heard Lorne's jangling earring. He was huddled at the bottom of the staircase with Max and Alvin. A worried frown had replaced his cherubic smile. His head swung back and forth in the universal language for no, the golden hoops of his earring jangling in mutual protest.

"Are you crazy?" he demanded, his voice rising to a high-pitched squeak. "It'll never work."

Alvin slouched against the railing and stared at Max as though he wanted to believe her but couldn't.

"It will work, I tell you," Max shouted. She stomped her foot on the bottom step of the stairs. Her red ponytail swung angrily back and forth. "Now hurry up!" she ordered. She grabbed Alvin's arm, pulled him off the stair step, and shoved him towards the elevators. "There's no time to lose."

"Alright, alright. I'm going," Alvin grumbled. He tugged his hat brim further over his face, slouched over to the elevators, and pushed the down button.

Lorne sighed deeply, and then followed Alvin. His head bobbled, his earring jangled. "Oh my. Oh my. Oh my. What if the captain finds out?" he muttered worriedly.

"Meet me in my room in five minutes!" Max ordered. She bounded up the stairs, her red ponytail bouncing wildly behind her. I bounded up after her.

Max didn't seem the least bit pleased to see me.

"Inspector Paws!" she exclaimed.

She scooped me up, hurried along the corridor, slid a card key into one of the many doors, carted me inside, and dumped me on the floor like a dirty shirt.

I lay where I'd landed and scanned my surroundings. I could tell by the surplus of shoes spilling out of the closet that it was Max and Stella's stateroom. It was larger than many of the rooms I'd glimpsed as I raced around the ship earlier in my initial search for Stella. A half-wall divided a portion of the room in two. One side featured a large king-sized bed with a fluffy comforter. The other side was set up like a small living room with a wrap-around sectional, a glass coffee table, and a large-screened TV.

Max strode past me, narrowly missing my tail, and flung the wall-to-wall sliding glass doors wide open. The salty tang of a brisk sea wind breezed into the room flapping the pages of the magazine on the coffee table and ruffling the hair on the back of my neck.

"Would you look at that sea, Paws!" Max exclaimed.

Look at it? Not if I could help it. The sound of it sloshing against the side of the boat was more than enough for me. I trotted into the bedroom portion of the room as far away from those open doors as possible, leaped into the middle of the king-sized bed, and sank into the softness of the fluffy comforter.

Max paced around the room in circles, taking quick peaks at her watch every two seconds

"Where is he? Where is he?" she muttered. Her ponytail flicked back and forth in annoyance.

Alvin had barely tapped on the door, when Max yanked it open, and pulled him inside, complete with his cumbersome and clattering trolley.

Alvin had changed into a pirate's costume. His red hair clashed with the bright red scarf tied in a knot above one ear. The black, sleeveless tunic, belted over a loose-sleeved white shirt, hung well below his knees. Tight leather pants, tucked into high-top boots sporting a wide cuff, completed his outfit. His former white uniform lay atop the trolley, all neatly folded. He lifted it off and clutched it to his chest.

"I don't know about this," he said. His face scrunched into a worried scowl. "If it doesn't work, my dad will kill us both."

"Then we better make it work, hadn't we?" Max replied. Her ponytail flicked defiantly. "You want to play in that pirate band, don't you?"

Alvin glanced down at his tall, laced boots and nodded. "Yeah, but ..."

"Then let's do it."

Max snatched the folded stack of clothing from his clutches and ran into the bathroom.

Ship's bells! She was going to put on Alvin's uniform and take his place as a room steward. And if I knew Max, she'd be doing some snooping while she was at it, probably in Leroy Garvey's cabin. Somehow I had to stop her. I raced into the bathroom after her and only just managed to pull my tail in before she slammed the door shut.

"We need to go over the list of things you have to do," Alvin called from the other room.

"Okay, talk," Max ordered. "I can hear you from here."

She slipped her feet out of her flip-flops and pulled Alvin's trousers on over top of her own leggings. They were too big. As soon as she let go of them, they slipped down around her ankles. Even when she threaded the belt through the loops and fastened it in the last notch available, the trousers slid past her hips. I purred in delight and wound myself around her feet. Surely now she'd abandon this idiotic plan.

I should have known Max wouldn't give up. She yanked the belt out of the bathrobe hanging on the back of the door, threaded it through the trouser belt loops, tied it in a tight knot, and tucked the stray ends inside her trousers.

"You're responsible for all the cabins on this deck," Alvin called from the other room.

"Okay," Max called back in a muffled voice as she pulled her tee-shirt over her head.

"You have to turn the bed down in each one," Alvin called. "I'll do this one so you know what to do."

"Okay," Max called. "I'll be right out and you can show me." She slipped her arms into Alvin's white jacket and fastened the brass buttons. If it weren't for her swaying ponytail, I could have sworn I was looking at Alvin.

Max stared at herself in the mirror. A look of puzzlement crinkled the freckles around her nose.

"Hey, Alvin," she called. "Why do you suppose we look so much alike?"

"Dunno," Alvin said. "Does it matter?"

Max shrugged, opened the bathroom door, and joined Alvin in the bedroom.

"Just wondering, that's all," she said. "I look like my mom, and you certainly don't look like your dad. What's your mother look like?"

"My mother's dead," Alvin said. His voice was sharp and abrupt as though he wanted no more questions.

"But what did she look like?"

Alvin scowled. "I don't know. Does it matter?"

"You don't know what your mother looked like? Don't you have pictures? What does your dad say about her?"

"My dad doesn't talk about her, okay? Now are you listening to what you have to do, or aren't you?" Alvin grabbed the narrow quilt that lay at the end of the bed. "You take this off and fold it like this." He neatly folded it and stashed it in a bin above the closet.

"Okay, I'm listening," Max said. She darted over to the closet, rummaged through it, and pulled out Stella's black wedge-heeled pumps. She slid a foot into one and hopped over to Alvin, pulling the other on as she hopped.

"Those are women's shoes," Alvin protested.

"Yours are way too big," Max said. "Besides, these have a higher heel. Keeps the hem from dragging on the floor. See." She stuck her foot out. "Besides, they'll be hidden by the pant leg. No one will see them."

Alvin groaned. "This isn't going to work."

"Of course it is," Max assured him. "So what else do I have to do?"

"You put one of these packages and a chocolate on each pillow." He paused and his face screwed up in another worried frown. "We're supposed to put a towel folded into the shape of an animal on each bed, too."

"Don't worry," Max said. "I learned how to do that at camp last summer. Now go." She dragged Alvin to the door and shoved him into the hallway, but he poked his head back through the doorway.

"You're not leaving your hair like that, are you?" he asked.

Max put a hand to her head. "The cap! I forgot the cap. Why do you wear that silly cap anyway?" she asked.

Alvin shrugged. "To annoy my dad, of course. Good thing, isn't it?" He grinned. "Otherwise you'd have to cut off that red ponytail of yours."

Max stuck out her tongue at him, but Alvin had already disappeared. The door closed behind him.

Max raced to the bathroom for the cap, but I'd already beat her to it. I grabbed Alvin's cap in my teeth, skidded through Max's legs, and raced for the open balcony. If I got rid of the cap, she'd have to give up the plan.

"Don't you dare, Inspector Paws," Max yelled from behind me.

I squeezed through the opening onto the balcony. Sea air whipped my face. I tried not to look at the swirling water. Six more inches and I could shove the cap under the railing and into the sea.

"You do, and I'll have to turn you in to the captain," Max yelled.

The captain? He'd lock me in the brig. I skidded to a halt. My head slammed into the glass of the railing.

Max snatched the cap out of my teeth, twisted her ponytail on top of her head, and pulled the cap over it. Her metamorphosis to Alvin was complete. There'd be no stopping her now. She grabbed the trolley and headed for the door.

"Wish me luck, Paws," she said as she pulled the door open.

Luck? She was going to need more than luck. I padded quickly across the room and slipped quietly onto the bottom shelf of the trolley.

CHAPTER 5

LEROY AND JO'S STATEROOM was even larger than Max and Stella's and twice as posh. The sofa wrapped around the entire corner of the room. I jumped onto it, and my paws sank into the soft leather. This would have been a perfect place to ride out this cruise if only it weren't in Garvey's cabin. He could walk through that door any minute. The thought made me shiver.

"Paws!" Max scolded. She dragged me off the sofa. "You're not supposed to be here. You'll get me in trouble."

Me get her in trouble? She didn't need my help for that. Instead of folding down the bed like Alvin had shown her, she headed straight for the desk and started rummaging through the drawers.

"Okay, Mr. Leroy Garvey, where are you hiding your dirty secrets?" she muttered.

Shiver me whiskers! Mad Max was hunting for dirt on Leroy Garvey. If he caught her, she'd be feeding the fishes in that deep blue sea. I knew stopping her would be next to impossible. Perhaps if I joined in the search, we'd find the dirt and get out of here before Garvey returned. I headed for the bedroom.

"Come here, Inspector Paws," Max called. "I need your claws to pry this briefcase open."

But my claws were already busy prying the closet door open.

Everyone knows skeletons are hidden in the closet. I'd just managed to create a crack big enough to squeeze through, when I heard a card key in the front door. The door banged open.

"Hey! What are you doing with my briefcase?" a man's voice demanded.

That wasn't Leroy's voice. Were we in the wrong suite? I sniffed at the bright red-and-white-checked snow boots. The puffy pompoms slapped against my nose. This was definitely Garvey and Jo's cabin. No one but Jo would wear boots like that, not even Stella.

"I was just dusting it," Max said. Her voice trembled slightly.

"Dusting it?" The man obviously didn't believe her. "Get out!" he ordered.

"But I have to turn down the bed," Max said.

"Out!" There was a definite threat in the man's voice. I cowered deeper into the closet. "Now!" The threat in the man's voice rose to new levels.

I could hear the trolley rattle noisily across the floor at an accelerated rate. The door banged shut. Ships bells! Max had left me here, stranded in Jo and Garvey's closet. If Garvey found me, I'd be the one feeding fishes at the bottom of the sea. Should I take my chances with the strange man who owned the briefcase?

Even as the thought crossed my mind, the front door opened, and Leroy's voice greeted the man.

"Angus. Would you look at this? Ruined. My favorite suit. Absolutely ruined."

"I'm afraid we have bigger problems than that, sir," Angus replied. "I just caught the room steward trying to break into my briefcase."

"What's your briefcase doing in here?" Leroy asked.

"I left it here so you could get Jo to sign those papers, sir.

Mike's moved the deadline up to the 20th. Have to start drilling soon so we can get it done before frost. Have you talked to her?"

Garvey burst into the bedroom.

I backed deeper into the closet and peered around the leg of one of Garvey's trousers.

The man called Angus trailed into the room behind Garvey. He was much younger than Garvey. Tall, dark and handsome would describe him well. In fact, too handsome, if you ask me. It was as though he wore a mask to hide his true nature.

"You know, Angus," Leroy said as he stripped off his white jacket with the bright pink stains and tossed it in the garbage can. "I don't even care anymore if she signs those papers. That woman is the best thing that's ever happened to me. Haven't had so much fun in years."

Ship's bells! Don't tell me Jo was a magician. Had she actually turned this toad into a charming prince? I couldn't quite shake off my doubts.

Leroy let his trousers fall to the floor and stepped out of them. Angus quickly turned away. I wished I could, but I didn't dare move. A portly man in boxer shorts, polka-dotted with neon pink hearts that sparkle in the sun, is not a pretty sight. They looked like something only Jo would wear. Maybe she'd given them to him. And maybe he really was in love with Jo. Surely, only a man in love would wear a pair of boxers like those.

"But sir," Angus objected. "We'll be out several million dollars if we don't get that property. We've already signed the drilling contract."

"Let's talk about it later, Angus." Leroy thumped Angus on the shoulder. "Got to go now. Jo's waiting for me. Signed us up for that honeymoon game. You know, the one where they ask all the questions. Hey! I've got an idea." He thumped Angus again.

Angus toppled onto the bed, his face buried in the soft duvet. He stiffly pulled himself upright.

"Why don't we make this a double wedding?" Leroy continued. "Me and Jo; you and Patricia."

Angus slid out from between Leroy and the bed and shuffled over to the closet. He glanced into the mirrored doors, smoothed his shiny, black hair, and straightened his tie.

"Just one problem with that, sir," he said. "Your daughter hasn't said yes yet."

Leroy shrugged. "She will. I have no intention of letting her marry anyone else."

Angus took a deep breath and smiled at himself in the mirror, smoothing the shiny black hairs of his moustache, much in the same manner as a cat who has just stolen a prime chunk of salmon from the kitchen counter.

"Where is Patricia, anyway?" Leroy asked.

Angus sneezed before answering.

"Downstairs talking to some woman she ran into. Apparently she writes those self-help books Patricia's so keen on." He sniffled as though suppressing another sneeze. "Turner, I think. Miriam Turner." He pulled the handkerchief out of his pocket and rubbed at his eyes. They'd turned quite red.

"Miriam Turner!" Leroy shouted. He advanced towards Angus as though he were about to strangle him. "You keep that woman away from Patricia, you hear? Those books of hers are filling the girl's head with all sorts of nonsense."

Angus tried to nod, but instead sneezed violently. His head banged against the closet door. I stuck out a paw to make sure it didn't close on me. Last thing I needed was to be trapped in the closet with no means of escape.

"What's wrong with you?" Leroy asked. "You're not coming down with a cold, are you?"

Angus rubbed his eyes again. "Allergies. If I didn't know it was impossible, I'd suspect there was a cat nearby. I'm deathly allergic to cats."

"Cats!" Leroy exploded. "Don't even mention cats to me!"

He flung open the closet door and yanked his suit off the hanger. I blinked up at him, totally exposed, nowhere to run. I did what any cat would do — puffed up my fur and hissed menacingly.

Leroy slammed the closet door in my face and ran for the living room.

"Get rid of him!" he yelled. "Get rid of that cat!"

"But sir, I'm allergic." Angus's voice trembled.

"I don't care if you're allergic," Leroy bellowed. "If you want to keep your job, you'll get rid of that cat!"

Angus slowly pried the closet door open with the tip of an umbrella. I backed behind another of Leroy's suits and hissed a warning. Stretching as far away from me as he could, Angus whacked wildly at the contents of the closet with his long-handled umbrella. Jo's red-and-white-checked snow boots flew out of the door, followed by a white crocheted dress. Leroy's silk tie slid off a hanger and wrapped loosely around my neck. I slid backwards trying to free myself, but my tail end rammed into the back of the closet. I lowered my ears, arched my back, hissed ferociously, and waited to grab that pillaging umbrella on its next swing, but the swing didn't come. Instead, Angus doubled over in a helpless fit of sneezing.

I streaked past him and raced into the living room. Angus dashed after me whacking wildly at everything he passed like a blind man on steroids, his eyes red, tears streaming down his face.

At the sight of me, Leroy leaped to the top of the coffee table and wrapped his arms around himself.

"Get rid of that cat!" he shrieked.

The coffee table creaked under his weight.

Angus's umbrella smacked into my hind end. I yowled, hissed, and slid under the sofa, but even that offered little refuge from the flailing umbrella. Angus knelt on the floor. The umbrella swung in wider and wider sweeps under the sofa. I slithered to the far end and peered out looking for somewhere else to hide.

The front door swung open, and the porcelain-skinned princess I'd seen talking to Miriam Turner entered.

"Hey, Daddy!" she called. "Guess who I met downstairs. Miriam Turner!" She waved her book in front of her. "And she signed my ..."

Her words choked to a stop. She stared at Leroy as he stood on the coffee table, the neon pink hearts on his boxers sparkling in the sunlight.

"Daddy? What are you doing?" she gasped.

I darted through her legs and into the hallway.

CHAPTER 6

THE HALLWAY WAS DESERTED. I trotted to the end of the corridor and peered around the corner. No sign of Max anywhere. Of all the dirty tricks. Not only did she desert me in Garvey's evil lair, but she didn't even wait around to rescue me once the coast cleared. I licked angrily at the side of my leg. Perhaps she was waiting in Max and Stella's stateroom. I hurried down the corridor and scratched hopefully on the door, but no one answered.

My tail swung back and forth in annoyance as I padded down the staircase. How was I supposed to keep Max and Stella out of trouble on this floating city in the middle of this whale-infested ocean when they kept disappearing? What I really needed was a place in the sun where I could stretch out, take an overdue catnap, and come up with a plan.

The pair of deckchairs tucked into a quiet alcove away from the giggling passengers seemed perfect. I jumped onto one of them, groomed every inch of my ruffled fur, and stretched out for my long-awaited nap.

A woman's high-pierced shriek dragged me awake. I jumped to my feet. The fur all over my body stood to attention. My back arched, and I hissed out a warning. The woman backed away, still screaming. A flash of white caught the corner of my eye as a crew member rushed toward me. I leaped off the chair, dashed through the doorway, and raced down the stairs. Perhaps the lower decks would be less crowded.

They weren't. People milled back and forth on every level, and from their reaction at the sight of me, you'd think they'd never seen a cat before. Didn't they know it was almost dinner time and they should be in their cabins getting ready?

I raced down six sets of stairs when I landed in a maze of shops. I knew the humankind were addicted to shopping. Why else would Stella have two suitcases full of shoes? But, ship's bells, bringing their shops along with them on vacation was above and beyond reason.

I strolled slowly down the corridor. There were shops of every description. One selling purses. One selling ladies' dresses. A counter in the middle of the corridor selling watches. Another with every sort of camera imaginable. Several jewelry stores. Even a shoe store. I slipped into this one and took a browse around in hopes of finding Stella, but with no luck.

A startled clerk made a dash for me, and I scooted out of there, raced down the rest of the corridor, and found myself in the casino.

Not one of the persons perched in front of the noisy, clanging machines bothered to look down at me. Their eyes remained firmly fixed on the ever-changing images that flashed across the screens, their hands fed a continuous stream of money into the hungry machines, and their feet drummed on the floor, keeping time to the booming bass of the loud music. If it hadn't been for the noise, I could have hid out in here all day, and no one would have ever noticed me. But how could a cat possibly think of a plan in the midst of all this chaos?

I tiptoed onward and was almost out of the casino when I saw my sun-worshipping admirer swaying back and forth on a stool in front of one of the noisy machines, still dressed in her scanty orange swimsuit. I tried to sneak past, but she looked down.

"Pussy cat! Pussy cat! Where've you been?" she slurred.

Before I could even move, she swooped down, nearly toppling off the stool, and scooped me into her lap.

"Come and give a poor lady some luck," she said.

I yowled in protest. I needed every ounce of luck I had. I couldn't afford to give any of it to her.

The woman pushed a few buttons on the machine in front of her, kissed the top of my head, nearly knocking me out with the fumes on her breath, and then thumped her hand against another button.

The machine went berserk. Lights flashed. Sirens sounded. Coins clattered into a metal tray, filling it, and spilling over onto the floor. The woman shrieked in delight.

"Money! Money! Look at all this wonderful money!" she slurred. She ran some coins through her fingers and then threw them in the air. "Who needs you Leroy bloody Garvey? A few more windfalls like that, and you can marry whoever you want!"

She toppled off her stool, taking me with her. Coins continued to spew out of the machine and rain down on our heads. The woman giggled drunkenly and scooped them close to her.

Yowling in terror, I picked up my tail and fled. I hoped I hadn't left all my luck with the giggling woman sprawled in her heap of coins, but I feared the worst when the corridor I chose came to a dead stop. I skidded into the large gold doors barring my way. Behind me the riotous noise of a pursuing posse rose to deafening heights. I could clearly here the now familiar shrieks.

"A cat! Catch that cat!"

Closed doors weren't going to stop me. I dug my claws under one of them, pried it open just a crack, and squeezed through.

The room, dark except for the eerie glow of a few pot lights, lay in a state of hushed expectancy. I eased further into the room. It was lined with seats set up in theatre style with a railing in front. I padded to the railing and peered over. A huge stage spread from wall to wall with two more tiers of seats just like these. I must have stumbled into the Nixes Theatre.

I jumped onto one of the seats and sank into the softness of plush velvet. My body curled into a purring ball. It would be hours until show time. There wasn't another soul in here. What better place to restore my frazzled nerves, catch up on a little sleep, and come up with a plan?

And perhaps I would have come up with that plan if I hadn't fallen into a deep sleep. I woke with a start when someone sat on top of me.

He was a young man in his early twenties with a mass of curly blonde hair encircling his head like an unruly halo, but the mischievous glint in his eye belied any thought of his being a perfect angel. He jumped up immediately and looked down at me with eyes as startled as mine.

I sprang to my feet ready to run, but the young man grinned at me and placed a hand on my back.

"No, sit," he said. He pushed my body back down into the curve of the seat, slid past me, and lowered himself into the seat beside mine. "I could use a pal to talk to."

A woman wearing too much makeup and a look of desperation seemed to think he was talking to her. "Me, too," she said. "Is that seat beside you taken?"

The young man shielded me with his program.

"Sorry," he said. "Can't you see my friend sitting here?"

The woman gave him the sort of look humans give those they think should be locked up for their own safety, and backed away. The lineup behind her also disappeared.

The young man laughed.

"There we are, then, Tiger," he said. "We've got the whole row to ourselves."

I was about to tell him my name wasn't Tiger, but decided this mischievous angel could call me anything he wanted. I stretched out on the seat and put a paw on his leg to show my approval. Here was a human almost as wise as Ernie.

"I'm Tyler Onslow," he continued. "And you must be the feline stowaway. Everyone's talking about you. Ooo! Lookie there." Tyler sat up straighter, peered over the railing, and whistled softly. "That's got to be the most beautiful girl on the ship."

I leaned over to see who he was looking at. Patricia Garvey walked through the large gold doors in the room below us, closely followed by her father and Jo. Patricia turned her head. Her long blonde hair swung around her shoulders like a beckoning flag.

"Oh, Daddy, you've just got to stop meddling in my love life," she said. Her long blonde hair flipped back and forth in anger. "Angus Lloyd is not the man for me. He's much too old, Daddy. He's stodgy, boring, and so unromantic. How could you possibly think I'd marry him?"

"You'll marry who I tell you to," Leroy Garvey ordered.

"Really, Daddy, this is the 21st century!" Patricia's voice rose in volume. "I'll choose my own husband." Her voice became dreamy. "I can picture him already. He's young, handsome, exciting."

"I told you to quit reading those silly books of Miriam Turner's. They're filling your head with all sorts of nonsense," Garvey barked.

"They're filling my head with dreams, Daddy," Patricia said.

"I can be anyone I want to be. I can do anything I want to do. I can marry who I want to marry."

"You have responsibilities, young lady," Garvey shouted. "You are my sole heir, and you'll marry someone who can look after you and your money in a responsible manner."

Jo hastily put a hand over Leroy's mouth. "Hush, darling," she said. "You'll have every fortune-hunter on the ship chasing after your daughter."

"Wow!" Tyler whispered beside me. "Not only beautiful, but rich, too." He gave another low whistle, and Patricia looked up at him with startled eyes. He touched his program to his glistening curls as though doffing his cap and smiled at her engagingly. Patricia blushed.

"Don't you even look at him," Garvey bellowed.

Jo tugged on Garvey's arm and ushered him to a seat right behind Stella, who was sitting far too close to the charming Captain Bonar for my liking. That prowling tom hadn't wasted much time, had he? I stifled the growl that threatened to give away my hiding place.

"Look who the lead singer is!" Jo exclaimed. She poked her program in front of Leroy's nose. "Berti Onslow!"

Onslow? I looked questioningly at Tyler. Wasn't that his last name?

"My mother," Tyler answered.

"Maybe we could get her to sing at the wedding," Jo said.

"Absolutely not!" Leroy exploded.

He tapped Captain Bonar on the shoulder.

"What's Berti Onslow doing on this cruise?" Leroy demanded.

Captain Bonar looked over his shoulder at him. "Last minute switch," he said. "We were lucky to get her. Singers of her caliber don't often appear on cruise ships." He arched an eyebrow. "Don't tell me," he said. "This ship isn't big enough for both you and her?"

"You've got that right," Garvey barked. "I've half a mind to call a chopper and get off this boat right now!"

I jumped to my feet. Could it be as easy as this? Was the man about to leave the ship?

Tyler's hand shoved me back down.

"Careful, Tiger," he said. "The bar boy will see you. Not everyone's as keen on feline stowaways as I am."

I sank back into my seat and watched Jo calm Leroy down.

The lights in the room dimmed, and the huge curtain on the stage lifted to reveal a motley band of musical pirates. Alvin stood at one end, his foot on a fallen barrel, his hands sliding up and down a guitar. He glanced nervously at the captain, but Captain Bonar didn't seem to recognize him.

They'd just finished their number when Lorne Akito bounced onto the stage. His head bobbled. His dangling earring jangled loudly. He, too, wore a pirate's costume, but instead of a guitar, he wielded a sword.

"Ahoy, me hearties!" His voice boomed over the crowd. His head bobbled with laughter. "Meet the Pirates of the Inside Passage! I and my crew have taken over this fine ship, and we'll give you a cruise you won't soon forget!"

His hearty laugh was echoed by everyone in the room — everyone except Leroy Garvey.

Garvey jumped to his feet. "Lorne Akito!" His shout cut through the laughter.

"Aye!" Lorne shouted back. "Lorne Akito at your service. Cruise director extraordinaire! And you're Leroy Garvey, the lucky bridegroom. What a wedding I've got planned for you!"

"No!" Leroy shouted. He shoved past Jo. "That man will have nothing to do with our wedding."

He strode down the aisle towards the rear door. Jo hurried to catch up to him.

"Shiver me timbers, but this is a tough crowd," Lorne declared. "They're already walking out." He laughed, but a tinge of concern shadowed his eyes as he watched Leroy and Jo rush toward the exit.

Before I had time to ponder Leroy's strange reaction to Lorne Akito, my sun-loving admirer bounced onto the stage. The audience went wild with applause. The woman had exchanged her scanty orange swimsuit for a pirate's costume. Her gauzy white shirt with the flowing sleeves, left practically unbuttoned to show off her ample bosom, was cinched in at the waist by a wide red leather belt fastened with laces at the front. Her black leather pants fitted like a second skin and were tucked into high-heeled, red boots that must have Stella drooling with envy. Her mop of unruly blonde curls, even though hers were bleached blonde, left no doubt that this was Tyler's mother.

I glanced at Tyler. He'd already slouched further into his seat.

"Hey, Leroy!" the woman shouted, her voice still somewhat slurred. "Don't leave on my account."

She twirled to the center of the stage carrying a full martini glass in each hand and not spilling a drop. She handed one to Lorne Akito and held the other at arm's length in the general direction of Leroy's retreating back.

"A toast to the dearly departed!" she called out and downed her drink. "Oh I do believe this is going to my lucky cruise." She slapped Lorne on the back. "Don't you agree, matey?"

Beside me, Tyler groaned. He peered at me from behind the program he'd used to cover his face. "A little over the top, isn't she?" he said. "Gets a tad embarrassing at times, if you know what I mean."

I knew exactly what he meant. I looked over at Stella.

She was laughing and clapping along with everyone else. The captain whispered something in her ear. She tilted her head back and looked up at him. The fur on the back of my neck stood on end. That was Ernie's look. She never looked at anyone like that. Not since Ernie died. How dare she give that look to anyone but Ernie?

I sprang to the railing. Ignoring my new friend's protests, I dropped to the floor below and landed with a splat on the armrest between Stella and the captain.

CHAPTER 7

AND WHAT DID MY ill-advised acrobatics accomplish? Nothing more than bruised ribs and a speedy pass to the ship's brig. In fact, I'd played right into the captain's hands.

The brig, hastily assembled by the crew, had once been a jewelry display case. They'd simply replaced all the glass with stainless steel grid work. I poked a tentative paw through the grid and fiddled with the catch, but it was securely locked. I knew the key was stowed in the inside pocket of the captain's jacket.

"Afraid our real brig is reserved for delinquents of the human variety," the captain said when he tossed me in here and turned the key in the lock. That easy smile of his had spread from ear to ear as he tucked the key into his inside pocket.

He said he was doing me a favor when he wheeled my cage to a prime spot in front of the floor-to-ceiling windows that graced his own quarters. Perhaps he truly thought it was a favor —I'll give him the benefit of the doubt — but the expanse of restless, rolling sea made my head spin and my stomach churn. I quickly turned my back on it and glared at the captain. He and I both knew why he'd put this "brig" in his quarters. Stella would be trotting in here two or three times every day to check on my well-being. He was simply using me as widow bait.

With its warm glowing wood, sparkling brass fixtures, and

soft leather seating, there was no doubt the captain's lair had been especially designed for luring unwitting widows. A glass and metal staircase spiraled up to what I assumed was the bridge, and tucked beneath it was a fully-equipped bar with bottles of various shapes glittering on the shelves.

The captain poured himself a tumbler of scotch whiskey, moved over to his desk, and flicked open a file.

The rich wooden bookshelves behind his desk made me think of Ernie's study. I looked longingly at the burgundy leather recliner. I could picture Ernie stretched out in it, a book in one hand, a glass of wine in the other, his Jesse Cook music filling the room. The only thing missing was the fireplace.

I sighed and rested my head on my paws. There was no point wishing for Ernie. Ernie was gone, and I was stuck here with the captain.

The captain wasn't about to relax in a recliner with a good book. He was parked in the corner, his chair tilted back, his feet propped on the desk like a pair of paper weights. He hadn't even opened the file tucked under his feet. He swirled his tumbler of scotch in his hand. The ice clinked unceasingly against the edge of the glass like some sadistic torture ritual.

A rap at the door brought a reprieve from the torture.

Captain Bonar sprang to his feet. His chair banged back in place. He hurried across the room and yanked the door open.

Great furry hairballs! I pressed my nose against the bars of my cage and gaped in amazement. I thought Jo was the queen of bizarre costumes, but Lorne Akito had her beat by far. He stood in the doorway dressed in a new pirate's costume that would make Jo look absolutely boring. His bright green tunic, canary yellow shirt with its billowing sleeves, and bright red head scarf made him look more like a parrot than a pirate.

He entered the room with much less boldness than his costume.

"You wanted to see me, sir?" he asked.

"I did." Captain Bonar ushered him in, poured him a glass of scotch, and the two of them perched at the bar swirling their drinks. The torturous ice clinked against the glasses in unison.

"I've had a complaint about you," the captain said.

Ships bells! Just one complaint? It's a wonder the whole ship hadn't risen in mutiny at the sight of that costume.

"From Leroy Garvey, no doubt," Lorne said. It was a statement not a question. He rested his elbows on the counter and rubbed his face with his hands. His earring jangled in sympathy.

Captain Bonar nodded.

Well if that wasn't the cat calling the baboon hairy! Hadn't I just seen Garvey perched on a coffee table flaunting his boxers with the neon pink hearts? What right did he have to complain about Lorne Akito's crazy costume?

"I suppose he's ordered you to sack me," Lorne said.

Captain Bonar nodded again. "I got the impression he'd rather I tied an anchor to your ankles and dropped you overboard."

Throwing a man overboard for wearing the wrong outfit? That seemed a little extreme, even for someone like Leroy Garvey.

Visions of Jo's outfits flashed through my mind — her red-and-white-checked snow boots with the puffy pom-poms, her sunhat that was so wide it pruned every tree she walked past, her wetsuit with the built-in flotation device that made her look like a blimp. What if Garvey took a dislike to one of her outfits?

"I hope you told him walking the plank was a thing of

the past," Lorne said. He gave a rather weak imitation of his infectious laugh. His earring barely tinkled.

The captain didn't even smile. "So what's the story?" he asked.

Lorne swirled his glass slowly and looked down at his feet. "I worked for him once," he said. "Must be a good five or six years ago. I headed up the human resources department. Garvey ordered me to fire a young single mom just before Christmas — an excellent employee. Her only fault? She refused to go out partying with the man." Lorne twirled his glass with increased vigor. The ice clinked furiously. "He gave me an ultimatum — fire her or be fired — so I quit."

"And he's still holding that against you?" Captain Bonar asked. His brow creased in a frown of disbelief.

"Garvey is not the sort of man to forgive and forget," Lorne replied. "He'll do everything in his power to destroy anyone who doesn't do what he wants."

Cat-o-nine-tails! What was Jo getting herself into? Jo wasn't the sort to let someone tell her what to do. It was only a matter of time before she did something Garvey didn't like.

Lorne Akito downed the last of his drink and pushed himself off the bar stool.

"Guess I'd better go pack, then, sir," he said. "Do you want me to leave the ship at Juneau?"

Captain Bonar sprang to his feet, a look of determination on his face. "You're not going anywhere, Akito," he said. "Except back to your duties."

"But sir," Lorne protested. His billowing yellow sleeves flapped wildly; his head bobbled; and his earring struck up a jangling protest. "You're asking for trouble if you don't do what Garvey wants," he said."

"I'll take my chances," the captain replied. His jaw tightened.

"I don't cow-tow to the likes of Leroy Garvey," he said. He strode over to the window, swiveled, and strode back. Picking up his glass of scotch, he swirled it angrily. The ice clinked alarmingly. "He's a brute and a monster. Just ask my sister," the captain added.

Lorne looked at him questioningly.

"Her husband, Clyde, worked for him once, too," the captain said. "Garvey not only fired Clyde, but he made sure he couldn't get a job anywhere else. Clyde killed himself. It happened years ago, but my sister's never been the same since."

Ship's bells! No wonder Miriam Turner didn't think this ship was big enough to share with Garvey.

Captain Bonar gulped down a swig of his drink, took a deep breath as though pulling himself together, and looked at Lorne Akito as though he'd forgotten he was in the room.

"That's all, Akito," the captain said. "Back to your duties."

"Oh, thank you, captain," Lorne gushed. He pumped the captain's hand. His flowing yellow sleeves flapped like wings. His earring jangled with pleasure. "I won't let you down, sir. I'll give the passengers a cruise they'll never forget, I promise."

Captain Bonar groaned. "Somehow that doesn't give me a great deal of comfort, Akito," he said.

Lorne headed for the door, his parrot's wings flapping wildly.

"And by the way," the captain called after him. "You're still on wedding duty. Seems Garvey's fiancé has talked him around."

"What?" Lorne stopped in astonishment. "Jo must be a wizard, or the man's truly in love. Nobody — and I mean nobody — has ever made that man change his mind."

Jo was a lot of things, but a wizard? I had my doubts. As for Garvey, I hadn't yet met a man who could change his character to that extreme. It was only a matter of time before Jo ran smack dab into the sharp edge of Leroy's ruthless anger, and then what would happen?

I clawed frantically at the hinges of my cage. I had to get out of here. I had to find Max. We needed to stop this wedding.

Great furry hairballs! Perhaps I was the wizard. Had my frantic thoughts drawn Max to the rescue? I could hear her outside the door.

"Come on," she said. Her impatience seeped under the door. "You want to know, too, don't you?"

Captain Bonar pulled the door open even before Max had a chance to knock. Max looked up at him in surprise. Her flipping ponytail slapped Alvin in the face. Max grabbed Alvin's wrist as though she feared he'd flee at any minute. Recovering from her surprise, she hauled Alvin into the room.

"Captain Bonar, we've come to find out about Alvin's mother," she said. She smiled up at the captain. "What did she look like? Did she look like us? I look like my mom. I just wondered if Alvin looked like his, and that our moms were related somehow."

She babbled on oblivious to the fact the captain's jaw had tightened ominously. Alvin tried to tug himself free. He'd obviously had more practice in reading the warning signs of the captain's displeasure.

"You have to admit it's uncanny how much alike we are," Max continued.

Captain Bonar drew a deep breath, closed his eyes, and kept them closed until he somehow managed to soften the look on his face. His frown disappeared, and his smile slid slowly back into place.

"Nonsense," he said. "Like I said before, everyone has a duplicate somewhere in the world."

Max was about to add to her argument, but the captain interrupted.

"I'm glad you dropped in, Alvin," he said, although his voice didn't sound all that welcoming. "I wanted to have a word with you."

Alvin tugged his baseball cap further down over his eyes and scowled up at the captain. "Why? What have I done now?" he asked.

The captain's jaw tightened again. "I had a call from Leroy Garvey," he said. He paused as though that should mean something to Alvin.

"So?" Alvin said.

"He says his assistant, Angus Lloyd, caught you attempting to pry open his briefcase."

"What?" Alvin slid his cap further back on his head so he could look into his father's eyes. "That's not true. When was I supposed to have done this?" he asked.

"Late yesterday afternoon."

Alvin glowered accusingly at Max, tugged his ball cap back down over his eyes, and shrugged. "He's paranoid," he mumbled. "Just dusting under it, that's all. So am I fired?"

"You'd like that, wouldn't you?" the captain said. He rubbed his face with his hands. "No. This calls for harsher punishment," he continued. "A little more work. A little less time to think about that guitar of yours. You'll help Lorne Akito with the Garvey wedding in addition to your other duties."

Alvin scowled and tried to tug Max toward the door. "Come on, Max," he said.

Ship's bells! They were leaving without me. I yowled loudly. Max looked at me, and then turned to the captain. I breathed a sigh of relief. She'd beg the captain to let me go with her. Surely the captain wouldn't be able to refuse Max's pleas.

Max looked up at the captain with that irresistible look of entreaty. "About Alvin's mother," she said.

The traitor! She wasn't thinking about me at all, only Alvin's mother. I pulled angrily on the bars of my cage and yowled even more loudly. Forget Alvin's mother!

Alvin echoed my sentiment. "Forget it, Max," he said. He grabbed her wrist, dragged her out of the cabin, and slammed the door behind them.

Captain Bonar stared at the closed door for a minute, and then ran his hands through his thick mane of white hair. He strolled over to my cage, although his eyes were on the sea behind me.

"Would you look at that sea, Inspector Paws," he said.

Not if I could help it. I buried my head in my paws.

"Perfect cruising weather," the captain continued. "Hardly a cloud in the sky. The sea's as calm as a sheet of glass."

Wasn't a sheet of glass when I'd last seen it — rippling with waves. I peeked over my shoulder. Not just rippling. Those waves sloshed back and forth like a churning washing machine, and my stomach sloshed back and forth with them.

"Wish the inside of this cruise ship were as peaceful." The captain again ran his hands through his thick mane of hair, which was every bit as wavy as the sea. "I'm afraid with Leroy Garvey aboard we'll be battling storm after storm after storm," he said.

A pod of whales dove past the boat blowing spouts of steam that shattered any image of a glass sea. Their tails slapped against the water. Flapping whales' tails! What was so peaceful about that?

Captain Bonar smiled.

"Perhaps I ought to toss him overboard and see if one of

those whales will swallow him," he said. "Isn't that what they did to Jonah when he was causing such a tempest?"

The captain was joking, of course. Wasn't he? I noticed the frozen stillness of his face as he gazed out at the sea. I shivered involuntarily. I wasn't cold, but every one of my whiskers quivered. Somehow I knew we hadn't even begun to see the extent of the trouble Leroy Garvey was about to cause on this cruise. Dread settled into the pit of my stomach like a stone. I sank to the bottom of the cage and rested my head on my paws.

CHAPTER 8

LEROY GARVEY EVEN HAUNTED my dreams. Jo, wearing her hat with the wide brim that pruned trees, had sliced a layer off the top of Garvey's bald head. He pulled an automatic rifle out of his back pocket and started firing at her, but Stella jumped in between them. Rat-a-tat. Rat-a-tat. The rifle's rapid fire increased in volume. Stella's shrieks increased with it. I had to help her, but I was locked in a cage. I struggled to get to my feet, but they slid out from under me. My head banged against the bars holding me in.

"Captain! Captain!" Stella's shrieks pierced my eardrums, but why was she calling for the captain? He wasn't her protector. I was.

My eyes popped open. This was no dream. Stella was pounding on the captain's door and screeching like a whole pack of sea monsters had hold of her tail.

I peered through the bars at Captain Bonar. He was sprawled across his couch like a sack of used clothing. His mouth gaped open. Baggy black bags circled his eyes. His hair stood up in tufts all around his head. Snores, even louder than Stella's knocking, shook his entire body.

Cat-o-Nine-Tails! Was this the man in charge of this ship? If only Stella could see him like this. One sight of this disheveled bum would surely wipe that stunned look of hero worship off Stella's face.

I clawed frantically at the bars of my cage, but it was no use. I'd need help to get out of here. I added my yowls to Stella's shrieks.

The captain snorted awake. He rubbed his eyes, looked first at me, and then stumbled over to the door and yanked it open.

"Oh, Captain," Stella said, nearly falling into the room. "You've got to help me."

Help her? She could come and go as she pleased, couldn't she? I was the one needing help. I banged my paws against the bars of the cage and yowled as loudly as I could.

Stella rushed over to me, cooing some sort of words that were supposed to calm me down, and stuck her finger through the bars. I slapped at her finger. I needed the key, not her bony finger poking at me.

Captain Bonar still stood in the doorway looking rather dazed.

"How'd you get in here?" he asked. He poked his head through the door and looked around the corner. "Where's the security guard?"

"Nursing a headache," Stella said without even looking at him. "Oh, Captain, please can't you unlock Paws's cage. Just let me cuddle him for a minute."

Captain Bonar looked at her blearily, yawned, ran both of his hands through his hair causing it to stand up in even higher spikes. Sighing deeply, he fished the key out of the inside pocket of his rumpled jacket and handed it to Stella.

"On your head be it," he muttered.

Stella needed no second invitation. She unlocked the door, slid me out of the cage, and clutched me to her chest, holding me so tightly I could barely breathe. And then she burst into tears, great body-shuddering sobs. Salty water slid down her face and dropped into my ears. Even the brig was more comfortable than this. I struggled to get free, but she only clutched me tighter.

"Hey, now, what's all this?" Captain Bonar asked. He guided Stella to a seat on the couch and sat beside her. His arms slid around the two of us.

Great furry hairballs! Cozying up to the rumpled, un-showered captain wasn't the way I wanted to start my day.

Stella didn't seem to mind, though. She rested her head on his shoulder and dabbed at her eyes with the sleeve of her sweater.

"I'm sorry," Stella sobbed.

The captain murmured some sort of words that even I couldn't understand and hugged us even tighter. I squawked out a complaint, but neither of them seemed to hear me.

"It's just that I'm so worried about Jo," Stella said. "I've heard even more rumors about Garvey since I've come on the ship. Jo's making a disastrous mistake marrying that man."

"There, there," the captain murmured. "Don't get yourself all worked up about it. Rumors aren't facts, you know."

"But your sister told me what he did to her husband," Stella protested. "He's a terrible man."

The captain tightened his grip on us.

Flapping whales' tails! How much more of this could a cat take? I gasped for air.

"Oh, Captain!" Stella wailed. "Can't you do something? Couldn't you stall the wedding? Say the papers haven't come, or something. Give me just a little more time to convince Jo this man isn't right for her."

The captain's grip loosened slightly. I gulped in some air while I had the chance. He reached for a tissue and dabbed at Stella's face.

"I know you're worried," he said. "But I really don't think it's our place to meddle. They'll sort it out. Garvey is pretty ruthless, but your friend Jo seems to be able to handle him. In fact, he seems willing to do anything for her. She'll be okay."

"That's just it." Stella sat up straighter on the couch. "Why is he doing anything Jo wants? It's not like him. Garvey has apologized to me twice just because Jo ordered him to. Patricia says that's unheard of. Her father never apologizes."

"Perhaps he really is in love with Jo," Captain Bonar said. He kissed the top of Stella's head. "Even wild beasts can be tamed by love, you know."

I nearly gagged up a hairball. The man was certainly playing it for all he could get.

Stella's hold on me loosened. I slid out of her clutches, dropped to the floor, and squished myself under the couch. She didn't even seem to notice I'd gone. She grabbed the captain's arm.

"He loves his daughter, too," she said. "But that didn't stop him yelling at her when she said she was going on the dogsled excursion with that nice young man who asked her."

"The dogsled excursion, you say? Hmm ..." Captain Bonar said.

He stood to his feet and paced back and forth for several seconds. Catching sight of himself in the mirrored shelves above the bar, he tried unsuccessfully to flatten the spikes of hair that sprouted from his head.

"Are Jo and Garvey going on the dogsled excursion?" he asked.

"Oh, yes," Stella replied, dabbing at her tear-stained face with a tissue. "Jo's all excited about it. Brought special outfits along for both of them."

"That's it, then," the captain said. He pulled Stella to her feet. "You and I will join them. Perhaps if we spend enough

time with them, we can draw out the real Leroy Garvey and let
Jo see him as the heartless scoundrel he really is."

I gagged up another hairball. It didn't take a flea brain to
see through that plan. All the captain wanted was more time
with Stella.

"Oh, Captain, I knew you'd come up with something." Stella
stood on her tiptoes and kissed the captain's bewhiskered cheek.

Another hairy fur ball clogged my throat. How could she
stand to get that close to his smelly breath?

I lowered my eyes and licked thoughtfully at my outstretched
paws. Stella was right about one thing though. We did need to
stop Jo from marrying the ruthless Garvey, but the captain's
self-serving plan wasn't going to solve anything. What we
needed was something tangible to show Jo.

A thought popped into my head. I sat straight up, bumping
against the bottom of the couch. What about those papers in
Angus Lloyd's briefcase? Could they be the evidence we needed
to convince Jo that Garvey was not the man for her? Angus had
certainly been anxious for Jo to sign them, and from the way
he'd wanted Garvey to put the pressure on Jo, they must be
something Jo didn't want to sign.

The door banged open and a frazzled crewman burst in.

"Are you okay, Captain?" he asked anxiously. "I tried to stop
her, but that tote of hers carries quite a wallop. Nearly knocked
me out."

He caught sight of Stella lost in the captain's embrace.

"Sorry, sir," he mumbled.

He slowly backed out the door, but not before I'd darted out
from under the couch, dodged between his legs, and escaped
into the hallway. I needed to find out what was in Angus Lloyd's
briefcase, and it was obvious I wasn't going to get any help from
those two.

CHAPTER 9

BY THE TIME I'D escaped the frenzied security guard, the ship was abuzz with twittering passengers flitting here and there, elbowing and shoving, trying to get the best place in the long lineup by the gangway. And all this just to get off the boat for a day in Juneau? Humans! There's just no understanding them.

Dodging the clumsy feet of excited passengers — sometimes unsuccessfully — I trotted up the stairs to Deck 10, limped down the corridor, and crouched, breathless and fur-ruffled, in front of the door to Garvey's suite. I still had no clear plan as to how I was going to find out what was in Angus Lloyd's briefcase. Was the briefcase still in Garvey's suite? And even if it was, how was I possibly going to claw my way into Garvey's suite?

I'd no sooner posed the question, than the door to the suite burst open, and Garvey himself appeared in the doorway. I jumped backwards and collided with a room steward's trolley parked outside the suite next to theirs. I slid onto the bottom tray and peered out from behind a pile of towels.

He wasn't parading around in his boxers with the neon pink hearts, but what he was parading around in was almost as shocking — tall black boots, puffy red ski pants, a bright red parka trimmed with white faux fur, and a matching long-tailed red toque. The parka fitted snuggly around his protruding paunch, which jiggled as he walked. He could have been Saint Nicholas himself if it hadn't been for the scowl on his face.

"Come along then, Jo," he said. "Let's get this over with."

"Oh, Leroy, don't be like that," Jo scolded.

She hurried out the door and grabbed his arm. She wore a matching outfit only her boots were the checked red and white ones with the matching pom-poms. One of the pom-poms slapped me in the face as she strode past the trolley, her arm in Garvey's.

"It's going to be fun," Jo said. She leaned her head onto Garvey's shoulder. "You'll see."

Garvey made a harrumphing sound that didn't sound the least bit encouraging.

"And you will be nice to Stella, won't you?" Jo asked. She looked at him anxiously. "You promised."

Garvey made another harrumphing sound. His belly jiggled as he dragged her around the corner to the bank of elevators.

I was just about to jump off the trolley when Alvin's angry voice burst out of the room I was parked beside.

"No! Absolutely not," Alvin barked.

"Aw, come on, Alvin," Max wheedled.

Great balls of fur! What was Max up to now? I huddled back behind the towels and perked up my ears.

Alvin raced through the doorway as though he were being pursued by demons. Max followed close on his heels. Alvin dumped several more soiled towels onto the lower shelf of the trolley. The stack tumbled on top of me, and the trolley, with me on it, clattered off down the hallway.

"Don't you even want to know about your mom?" Max pled.

"Get lost," Alvin ordered. He slid his card key into a slot and shoved the trolley into the room.

I slithered out from under the pile of towels and looked

around me, hardly daring to believe my eyes. He'd wheeled me right into Garvey's suite. Surely this was a sign. I was definitely on the right track. Now, if only the briefcase was still here.

Max hurried into the room before Alvin could close the door.

"Alvin, you've got to see this," she ordered.

She pulled her cell phone out of her pocket and held it out to him, but Alvin scooted away from her and disappeared into the bathroom with his cleaning supplies.

"I told you to get lost," Alvin said. "You shouldn't even be in here. Haven't you caused enough trouble?"

"But just listen to this," Max said. "I texted my mom and asked her if she had any relatives that married a man named Bonar, and here's what she said." Max's voice filled with excitement. *"My father's youngest sister married a Bonar, but we don't talk about her. Now stop meddling in things that don't concern you. I knew I shouldn't have let you go on that cruise with your grandmother."*

"She's right," Alvin said. He brushed past Max and disappeared into the bedroom with fresh sheets. "You shouldn't have come on this cruise. Now stop meddling."

"But don't you want to know?" Max asked. She followed him into the bedroom. "Why don't they talk about her? Why doesn't your dad talk about her?"

"You don't even know she's the same person," Alvin said. "And if you're not going to leave, the least you could do is help me make this bed."

"But you could help me find out if she's the same person," Max said.

"I told you to stop meddling."

Alvin dumped a pile of sheets on the trolley, once more putting me in the dark. I burrowed my way out from under them just in time to see Max's stubborn chin rise, and her red ponytail swing angrily.

"Alvin Bonar," she said. "If you don't help me find out about your mom, I just might have to let your dad know who that guitar-playing pirate in the band is."

Alvin dropped the handful of brochures he'd been laying out on the side table. They floated to the floor, and he knelt to retrieve them. He stood to his feet, carefully rearranged them on the table, and then turned to glare at Max.

"That's blackmail," he said.

"So what if it is?" Max said. Her chin lifted even higher. Her ponytail flicked behind her. "I need to know. I can't believe you don't want to know who your mother is. Surely you've got a birth certificate, or something. We can look it up on the internet."

Alvin switched on the vacuum cleaner drowning out anything further Max had to say. Max waited until he'd switched it off.

"You're just afraid," she accused. "You're scared you won't like what you find out."

"I am not scared," Alvin said. He tugged his ball cap lower over his eyes and stacked a couple of dirty cups onto the trolley. "Okay, okay," he said. "We'll look her up on the internet."

Max jumped in delight. Her ponytail flicked against a picture on the wall knocking it askew. Alvin hurried over to straighten it.

"We better use dad's computer," he said. "It's more private. And he'll be gone today. He's off on that dogsled excursion with your gran."

"Thank you! Thank you! Thank you!" Max shouted. "You won't regret this. I promise." She hugged Alvin, knocking his cap to the floor.

Alvin squirmed out of her embrace, retrieved his cap, plopped it back on his head, and tugged it low over his eyes. "I already do," he muttered.

Cat-o-nine-tails! Every one of my whiskers trembled in protest. If I read those trembling whiskers right, they were both about to regret this. Why couldn't Max leave things well enough alone? Had she forgotten she was here to keep Jo from marrying Garvey? Wasn't that enough trouble for her to get into?

"Seems to me your dad is getting awfully interested in my gran," Max said as she helped Alvin load the rest of the dirty dishes onto the trolley.

Alvin shrugged. "Dad's nice to all the women," he said. "He considers it his duty, part of his job."

Ship's bells! Hadn't I just seen him cuddling Stella like a tom grooming his would-be partner. Way above and beyond the call of duty, if you ask me. Another problem that needed clearing up, but not right now. I had just spied Angus Lloyd's briefcase tucked on the far side of the desk. I slipped silently off the trolley, slid under the couch, and waited for Max and Alvin to leave. Unlike Max, I could keep focused on the priorities, and the priority right now was to keep Jo from marrying Garvey. Hopefully that briefcase contained all the evidence we'd need.

CHAPTER 10

THE TROLLEY CLATTERED INTO the hallway with Alvin at the controls. Max followed him out, but the door slammed into her backside. She sprawled into Alvin, knocking both him and the trolley across the hallway.

"Be careful, would you?" Alvin grumbled. "You're going to get us in trouble."

I could have told him that Max thrived on "trouble".

I crawled out from my hiding place under the couch and padded over to the briefcase. I had my own trouble to pursue, and I was beginning to realize I once again hadn't given my plan enough thought. How was I going to get the briefcase open? I fumbled unsuccessfully with the lock, scratched on the fine leather, but nothing gave. And even if I did get it open, how was I going to get out of this suite with the evidence?

I heard the sound of a card key sliding into the door behind me. The hairs on the back of my neck stood on end. I tried to race for cover, but my claw caught in the clasp of the briefcase. Cat-o-Nine-Tails! Talk about being caught with your claw in the cookie jar.

Angus Lloyd burst into the room, strode across to the desk, and reached for the briefcase. He saw me, and his hand froze in midair. His eyes, already starting to water, bulged out of his face.

"The demon cat!" he hissed. "How'd you get in here?"

He slowly backed towards the door. I breathed a sigh of relief. With Garvey not here ordering him to get rid of me, perhaps he'd just back out of the room and run for help. That would give me time to get this briefcase out of here. I grabbed the handle with my teeth and tugged, but the briefcase was heavier than I thought. I freed my claw from the clasp and made another attempt.

"What kind of cat are you?" Angus Lloyd whispered, his eyes frightened as though he were looking at some spirit risen from the sea. He sneezed violently, and then flapped his hands in my direction.

"Shoo! Scat! Get away from that!" he ordered.

He backed further away, but instead of leaving the room as I'd hoped, he grabbed a duffel bag off the couch, unzipped it, and flipped it upside down. A couple of pairs of black leather pants, a ruffled white shirt with billowy sleeves, a black hat decorated with a skull and cross-bones, and a black eye-patch tumbled into a pile on the floor. In one fluid motion, Angus Lloyd slid across the room and plopped the empty duffel bag over my head.

Hissing, growling, and spitting, I clawed at the bag trying to free myself, but Angus Lloyd flipped the bag upright. I tumbled to the bottom, my feet clawing the air. Before I could even get my breath, he zipped the bag closed. He sneezed violently three times in succession. Each sneeze joggled me up and down like a yo-yo.

"You know what happens to spying stowaways, don't you?" Angus said.

He sounded more confident now that I was firmly trapped in this bag. He strode across the room. I could hear the balcony doors slide open.

"They walk the gangplank," he said. He chuckled villainously, and then bent over in another fit of sneezing. "Garvey will owe me one for this," he said. He sneezed again, violently joggling me up and down. "If you're lucky," he continued. I could feel him lift me high into the air. "This bag might even float."

And then I was falling.

I yowled as loudly as I could, but of course there was no one to hear. I wondered how long it would take to hit the water. I tried not to think about those turbulent waves waiting to swallow me. I tried not think about how cold that icy water would be. I tried not to think about the whales spouting air like salty tea kettles or all those other monsters waiting in the dark depths of the ocean. I closed my eyes and waited for the splash.

Instead of a splash, I landed with a thud that shook my rib cage.

"What was that?" Stella asked.

Stella? What was Stella doing here? I tried to yowl, but I couldn't get my breath. The squeak I managed wasn't audible above the chugging engine of the boat I'd landed on top of. It must be one of the tenders taking the passengers to shore for their excursions.

"That's your duffel bag, Leroy!" Jo exclaimed. She sounded like she couldn't believe what she was seeing.

"Nonsense," Garvey said. "What would my duffel bag be doing flying through the air? I'm sure there's lots of bags like that."

"But it's yours," Jo insisted. "Can't you see those neon pompoms? I tied those on myself so we'd recognize it among all the other luggage? Oh, do grab it, Leroy."

The boat tipped from one side to the other as Garvey moved below.

"Can't reach it," Garvey grunted. "Let it go. It's just a bag."

"But it's got our costumes in it — the ones for the masquerade ball," Jo protested.

"I'll get it," Captain Bonar said. "I'm taller than you."

The bag started to slide. I clawed frantically, trying to grip onto something, anything to keep from falling into the icy water.

"What the ...!" Captain Bonar shouted, obviously startled by my frantic contortions.

He yanked on the bag, but it slid out of his hands.

The splash was everything I'd dreaded. The chill of the icy water seeped through the bottom of the bag and crept between my toes. Captain Bonar had just completed Angus Lloyd's mission. I was about to find out what was in Davey Jones's locker. I yowled so loud the hairs on my own head stood on end.

"Paws!" Stella shrieked. "Paws is in that bag. Out of the way!" she ordered.

"No, Stella, you can't jump in!" Captain Bonar shouted.

"Let me go!" Stella shouted back. I could hear her desperation even as her voice drifted further away.

"I'll get him," Captain Bonar assured her. "But not like that."

His voice, too, had drifted further away, and my hopes of rescue drifted with it. The icy water had numbed my feet and crept steadily upward chilling the rest of my body. My teeth rattled together making it hard to yowl for help.

"Turn the boat!" Captain Bonar's distant shout barely reached my ears, but in a few minutes something latched onto the bag. I felt myself rising out of the sea. Water cascaded off my bag like an upside down whale spout. I breathed deeply as Captain Bonar hauled me aboard the tender, unzipped me from the bag, and tucked me safely into Stella's warm parka.

"You did this," Stella said. She looked accusingly at Garvey.

"Me?" Garvey eyed me warily and tried to back as far away from me as he could, but he was already at the edge of the boat. Any further and he'd be the one swallowing salty water. "I didn't do anything," Garvey protested. "I was here with you."

"Of course you didn't do it yourself," Stella said. Her arms tightened around me. "You ordered that assistant of yours to do it for you."

"Oh, Leroy, how could you?" Jo asked. She too looked at him accusingly.

"But I didn't," Leroy protested again.

Jo held up a hand as though trying to stop him from speaking.

"There's no need to lie about it, Leroy," she said. "We all heard you order the captain to throw Paws overboard. I just didn't think you really meant it." Her brown eyes filled with tears of reproach.

Was Jo finally beginning to see Garvey as he really was? Perhaps my close call with the monsters of the deep had been worth it after all.

I snuggled closer to Stella, my rumbling purrs falling into rhythm with her throbbing heartbeat.

CHAPTER 11

I COULDN'T HELP FEELING even more pleased with myself when Stella told the captain she'd forego the dogsled excursion and take me back to the ship. I'd not only driven a wedge between Garvey and Jo, but my very presence was about to keep the captain from getting his paws on Stella. I licked Stella's chin and gave the captain a smug look, but my self-congratulation soon evaporated.

"No need for that," the captain said. "We'll just take him along with us."

Cat-o-Nine-Tails! They weren't taking me on any wild ride with a pack of raving dogs. I tried to squirm out of Stella's clutches, but she tucked me firmly into her parka and zipped it tight.

The least she could have done was argue with the captain, but no, she seemed traitorously delighted at the prospect. She grabbed the captain's arm and skipped along beside him as he dragged us both into the belly of one of those flying birds with the rotary blades that make enough noise to burst a cat's eardrums. Could things get any worse?

Apparently they could. Garvey's bellowing voice greeted us.

"I forbid it!" he bellowed.

I poked my head out from Stella's parka. Was my arch-enemy

Garvey going to be my unwitting rescuer? But Garvey wasn't looking at me at all. He was looking at Patricia.

Patricia, seated in the front seat of the helicopter, snuggled closer to Tyler Onslow, her fairy-like locks mingling with his messy blonde halo.

"There's no use shouting at me, Daddy," Patricia said. She looked up at him defiantly. "I'm over eighteen now. Old enough to make my own decisions. I'll choose my own friends."

Garvey, his face every bit as red as his tight-fitting Santa Claus suit, leaned threateningly over her.

"You're not going anywhere with him!" he yelled. "He's nothing but a fortune hunter!"

Tyler put a protective arm around Patricia and grinned nervously at the shouting Garvey.

"Chill out, man," Tyler said. "I'm not eloping with her. Just taking her on a dog sled ride."

He caught sight of me tucked into Stella's parka and seemed to leap at the chance to distract the seething Garvey.

"Hi, there, Tiger!" Tyler said. "Don't tell me you're coming with us."

Garvey turned to see who Tyler was talking to. His eyes widened. He backed hurriedly down the aisle of the chopper.

"The cat! Get rid of that cat, Captain!" he ordered, his voice a mere squeak.

I flexed my claws and hissed at him.

He toppled into the seat beside Jo, and she quickly buckled him in. Scowling at Stella, Jo tried to calm Garvey and keep him buckled in his seat.

The helicopter tilted, tossing both me and Stella against the window. I forgot all about Garvey as I saw, spread out below me, my own worst nightmare. A dog town! Row upon row of white dog houses, and beside each cookie-cutter dog house stood a drooling dog with an eagerly wagging tail. At the sound of the helicopter, the dogs clambered to the roof of their houses and looked upward as though they expected dog food to fall from the sky. Had they already caught my scent?

I cowered back into Stella's parka.

No one else seemed to dread getting off the chopper and entering the town of dogs. Tyler and Patricia bounced off, laughing gleefully, and raced for one of the waiting sleds already harnessed to a team of yelping dogs.

Great tufts of dog hair! How could they possibly think this was fun? Humans! There was just no understanding them.

I buried my nose deep into Stella's parka to escape the fetid stench of dogs' breath, but no matter how deep I burrowed into the fake fur of her collar, I couldn't escape the chilling sound of their panting and their blood-thirsty baying. It rose into the air like the spine-chilling chords from some horror movie.

Stella must have felt me tremble underneath her jacket. She patted me soothingly.

"Oh, Paws, I'm sorry. We shouldn't have brought you," she moaned.

I yowled in agreement, and the dogs set up an even more frenzied barking and snarling at the sound of my voice.

I peered warily out from the shelter of Stella's partly unzipped parka. Captain Bonar had already climbed onto the runners of one of the sleds and was beckoning Stella and me to crawl into the sled itself. The dogs pranced and lunged at the front of the sled. Saliva dripped from their dangling tongues making pockmarks in the snow. They yelped noisily as though daring us to climb aboard.

Garvey bellowed from behind us, and I nearly jumped out of Stella's arms.

"Patricia Garvey, you wait for me!" Garvey roared. "You're not going off alone with that fortune hunter."

Patricia leaned back into the sled, as though she were Cinderella on her way to a ball. She waved prettily at her father, and then blew him a kiss.

"See you later, Daddy," she called.

Tyler, standing on the runners behind her, laughed.

"Mush! Mush!" he ordered.

The dogs needed no second invitation. They howled and lunged forward. Patricia shrieked in delight.

"Out of my way!" Garvey bellowed.

He shoved Stella sideways. Her feet slid out from under her, her hands flew into the air, and I flew right out of her arms. I landed with a body-jarring thud that bruised my ribs and left me, not only breathless, but just whiskers away from the lead dog of the sled Captain Bonar had boarded. I yowled in terror. The dog's eyes bulged. His mouth widened. His tongue dangled so low it nearly touched the snow. His grin spread from ear to ear. He howled in excitement and headed straight for me.

Slobbering dog drool! Forget the bruised ribs. I had to get out of here.

I picked myself up off the snow, somersaulted away from him, and ran as though a whole pack of hungry wolves were chasing my tail. And for all intents and purposes, they could well have been a pack of wolves. They bayed and brayed in hot pursuit, their chains rattling, as they got ever closer. Captain Bonar's frenzied shouts of "Whoa! Whoa! Stop!" didn't slow them in the least. At this rate, they'd be chewing my tail in a matter of seconds. I lifted that appendage even higher and picked up speed, trying desperately to spot somewhere, anywhere to hide. But there was nothing but snow all around me.

And then I saw Garvey's sled. I was gaining on it with each

renewed burst of speed. Garvey stood on the runners like a frenzied Santa Claus totally out of control, the long red tail of his toque flapping wildly behind him. He cracked a whip against the icy snow bank and bellowed at the dogs.

"Move it, you mongrels!" he yelled. "Catch that sled!"

He was obviously trying to catch up with Tyler and Patricia.

He certainly wasn't my first choice for a safe haven, but beggars can't be choosers. If I could get into that sled, those wolves behind me would have to get through Garvey before they could get to me. If it came to a contest between Garvey and the raging dogs, I'd bet all my whiskers on Garvey any day.

I dug deep for an extra burst of adrenaline, sped past Garvey, carefully avoiding his cracking whip, and with a leap born of desperation, I landed in the sled.

My plan hadn't allowed for Garvey's fear of the cat. It was even greater than my fear of a pack of raging dogs. His shout of terror soared above the frenzied baying of the approaching dog pack.

"Out! Out!" he shrieked.

His whip cracked in my direction, nearly shaving off one of my ears. I dove to the bottom of the sled and slid under the seat for safety. Garvey's whip continued to beat the chair above me. Dust and debris rained down on my head and embedded itself in my fur.

With each crack of the whip, Garvey's other hand jerked on the left handle of the sled. The dogs spun left, and then left, and then left again. The sled spun in ever narrowing circles. I dared a peak out from under my hiding spot. I could see what was about to happen even before it did.

Captain Bonar's dogs were nearly upon us. Captain Bonar yanked backwards on the runners.

"Whoa! Stop!" he yelled frantically.

But the dogs sped toward us, barreling into Garvey's frenzied dogs. The two packs of dogs turned on each other, snarling, growling, a fight to the death.

I tried to jump for safety, but it was too late. The sled flipped. I sprawled under it, my nose jamming into the cold snow, and listened to the wailing, baying, snarling dogs above me, and the screaming curses of both Garvey and Captain Bonar.

It took several hours for the dogs' trainers to untangle the mess of snarling dogs and get them back under control, but it would take more than dog trainers to get Garvey and the captain under control.

Captain Bonar dragged me out of the wreckage, somewhat less than sympathetically, clamped me in a vise-like grip, and hauled me back to Stella, but when Stella reached for me now gushing and cooing with a far-too-late show of concern, the captain shoved me roughly inside his parka, zipped it shut, and squished me so tightly against his chest I could barely breathe.

"I'll hang on to him," he said. "Safer that way."

Safer for whom? I yowled. Had I escaped a pack of wild dogs only to be squished to death in the arms of a sea captain?

I tried another yowl for help, but my pathetic mewl was drowned out by a tirade from Garvey.

"You haven't heard the last of this, Captain Bonar!" Garvey shouted.

The whole town full of dogs bayed in agreement.

Garvey shifted the icepack on his forehead.

"Don't think your superiors won't hear about this!" he yelled, and then winced in pain.

Jo tried to calm him.

"Now, Leroy, yelling isn't going to help," she said.

She finished binding his sprained arm into a sling and tried to move him towards the helicopter.

"And besides," Stella butted in. "It wasn't the captain's fault. He didn't run into you on purpose. If you hadn't shoved me, none of this would have happened."

Jo turned on Stella before Garvey could even respond.

"And if you hadn't brought Paws, Stella, none of this would have happened."

"It wasn't my idea to bring Paws," Stella said. "Your beloved Garvey was the one who tossed him overboard, remember? Tried to kill him."

"I did no such thing!" Garvey yelled. He winced again and once more covered his head with the icepack.

"You probably arranged that, too," Jo said. "You and Max. You probably had Max throw Paws overboard in Garvey's duffel bag, just to stir up trouble for Leroy. You planned all of this, didn't you?"

"Stop it! All of you!" Captain Bonar's commanding bark brought the group to an uneasy silence. Even the dogs ceased their braying.

"Let's get back to the ship," the captain said. "Before anyone says something they'll regret."

He herded the group onto the chopper without another word. In fact, no one said a word for the rest of the trip back to the ship, but the air bristled with unspoken violence.

Even the sky darkened. Thick billowing clouds scudded across it. A brisk wind picked up the helicopter and tossed it up and down.

I hunkered deeper into the captain's parka. It seemed the storms the captain had predicted were about to break both inside and outside the ship.

CHAPTER 12

"I DON'T KNOW ABOUT you," the captain said. "But I could use a drink."

I yowled in agreement. And some food. But of course he wasn't talking to me. He shoved me deeper inside his parka and held out a hand to help Stella out of the tender and back onto the ship.

"Oh, what a great idea," Stella said.

No surprise there. Stella was always up for a drink.

"Looks like our little plan didn't work so well, did it, captain?" Stella said. Her face screwed up in disappointment. She tucked her arm into the captain's and leaned her head against his shoulder.

Great furry hairballs! Did the woman have no sense? Captain Don Juan didn't need any encouragement. I tried to squirm out of the captain's parka and shove her away from him, but the captain's grip on me tightened.

"Oh, I don't know," Captain Bonar said. "At least Jo saw a side of Garvey she didn't like."

"Doesn't seem to have bothered her much," Stella said. She scowled as she looked over at the bank of elevators where Jo and Garvey stood hand-in-hand waiting their turn. "And she's blaming me for Garvey's ill temper. You heard her. She's blaming me for everything. Thinks Max was the one who tossed Paws down in Garvey's duffel bag. That it was all planned. Oh, I do wish Paws hadn't followed me onto this ship."

That made two of us. I pulled my head down further into the captain's parka so I no longer had to look at the ungrateful traitor. What's a cat got to do to get a little appreciation? Hadn't I risked one of my nine lives to help her out? And that's all the thanks I get.

Captain Bonar undid his parka and pulled me out of my hiding place.

"All right then, little trouble maker," he said. "Let's get you back to the brig."

I hissed my disapproval, but both of them ignored me.

"See you in the Club Lounge in 15 minutes, Stella," the captain said as he strode off towards his quarters.

As soon as the captain opened the door to his quarters, we could hear a woman singing. The captain's hand froze on the door handle. Obviously he wasn't expecting visitors. His grip on me tightened.

The woman's voice rose, filling the air with melancholy anguish, as she crooned about a lost lover.

"She was a singer!" Max's excited voice rose above the sounds of the woman's pain. "Alvin, can you believe it? Your mother was a singer! My great aunt was a singer!"

"And a good one," Alvin replied, his voice hushed with admiration.

"But why won't they talk about her?" Max asked. "My mom said her family won't discuss her. Your dad won't talk about her. What do you suppose she did?"

"I'll tell you what she did," Captain Bonar said. The harshness in his voice sent a shiver up my spine.

Both Alvin and Max jumped. They were huddled in front of the captain's computer screen, where a young woman, who looked a lot like Max, with freckles and a long red ponytail, continued to bewail her lost love.

The captain's vise-like grip on me tightened even more as he stepped further into the room.

"She killed herself. That's what she did," Captain Bonar said.

Alvin's eyes widened in shock.

Captain Bonar held out a hand to him.

"Sorry, son," he said, his voice softening. "I shouldn't have said it like that. I just never knew how to tell you."

He was about to say more when Garvey stumbled into the room already in midsentence.

"Glad I caught you, Captain," he babbled. "Jo made me come. Said I had to apologize. I got a little out of control today."

Garvey caught sight of the computer screen, and his eyes widened.

"Nola Davis!" he said. "That's Nola Davis."

He pushed his way past the captain and stared closer into the screen.

"I'd forgotten how good she was," he said.

He threw an arm around each of Max and Alvin and leaned even closer to the screen.

"I helped that young lady get her start, you know," Garvey said. His voice pricked with pride. "I met her at a karaoke bar in Toronto. Told her she ought to go professional, but she was married to some deadbeat husband who wanted her to be the little woman, look after the house and the kids. So I gave her the money to go out on her own, do her own thing."

He shook his head in amazement as the woman's voice drifted into the final notes of her song.

"Shame she got into the drug scene, though," he said, shaking his head ruefully. "Ended up with a fatal overdose."

The woman finished her song, bowed low, and smiled into the camera.

"Oh, my God!" Garvey exclaimed. He looked at Max and then at Alvin. "She's a spitting image of you two."

He swung around. His startled eyes took in the captain's white face and frozen stance.

"You?" Garvey said. "You were the husband?"

Captain Bonar lifted one hand and pointed to the door.

"Out!" he said.

"But I didn't know," Garvey protested.

"Out!" Captain Bonar roared.

Garvey scurried past him and out the door.

Captain Bonar moved slowly towards the computer screen. The woman had started into a new song. This time her voice lilted to a Celtic melody of delight. Captain Bonar dumped me on the floor and sank into a chair in front of the screen.

"Couldn't you tell us a little bit about her, Captain?" Max asked.

Captain Bonar didn't answer. It was as though he didn't hear her.

"Captain," Max repeated. She raised her voice in an attempt to get his attention.

Alvin tugged on Max's sleeve and tried to pull her toward the door.

"But don't you want to know about your own mother?" Max asked.

"Not now," Alvin said.

He yanked on Max's arm and dragged her out the door.

I quickly trotted after them. I stopped briefly in the doorway and glanced over my shoulder.

Captain Bonar sat with his elbows on his desk, his head resting on his hands, and stared at the screen, where his dead wife smiled into the camera, her voice lilting like a fairy in flight.

CHAPTER 13

"AHOY, ME HEARTIES! THIS is your cruise director speaking."

Akito's voice, booming out of the loudspeaker directly over my head, jolted me out of a deep sleep and a dream of better days, days when I was curled up in Ernie's lap in his chair by the fire listening to soft music. Akito's booming voice and jangling earring didn't fit into the dream at all.

I stretched, trying to remember where I was, and my claws dug into someone's chest.

Alvin jumped awake. His knee slammed into the back of the towel cart, and a stack of towels tumbled off, burying us both.

"Hey, watch those claws, would you?" he grumbled, digging us out from under the pile of towels.

I remembered now. After escaping the captain's quarters, I'd tried to get into Stella's cabin, but she wasn't there, probably waiting for her gallant captain in the Club Lounge. The sight of a white uniformed crew member had sent me scurrying for cover. I'd darted into a niche behind the cart of towels stacked beside the swimming pool, but it was already occupied. Alvin sat huddled there, his head buried in his hands. For once he'd seemed glad to see me. He scooped me into his arms, cuddled me close to his chest, and whispered into my ear. I guess he needed someone to talk to, and even a cat would do.

"So, Inspector Paws," he'd whispered. "What do you think of that? My mom was a singer. Can you believe it?" He rubbed his nose in my fur and cuddled me closer. "No wonder my dad doesn't want me chasing after music," he continued. "He probably thinks I'll end up on drugs, too, just like my mom. I won't you know. Don't want anything to do with drugs. Seen too many kids messed up on them to get mixed up in that scene."

He breathed in deeply and sat up straighter.

"But I've got to sing," he said. "I've got to play." His voice rose.

At this rate he'd be giving away our hiding place. I put my paws on his chest and tried to lick his mouth to keep him from saying anything more. He turned his face away, grabbed me in his arms, and stretched out full length. His voice lowered back to a whisper.

"Okay, okay," he whispered. "I'll be quiet. But I am going to sing and play, you know, no matter what my dad says."

We'd both drifted off to sleep, and now we both cringed as Akito's pealing laughter assaulted our ears. I tried to bury my head under Alvin's arm, but Akito's next words snapped my head back up.

"Please be on the lookout for a feline stowaway," he boomed.

"Feline stowaway?" Alvin murmured. He ruffled the fur on my head. "That must mean you, Inspector Paws."

"He's a fat cat, so shouldn't be hard to miss," Akito continued.

Fat? I looked down at the rolls on my midriff and pulled in my stomach. I wasn't fat. That was muscle — pure muscle.

Alvin chuckled and squished my rolls of muscle under his fingers.

"And a rather unusual cat," Akito continued.

Nothing wrong with that. I raised my head in defiance. Who wants to be a copycat?

"Not the least bit cuddly," Akito added.

That all depends who's doing the cuddling. I squished closer to Alvin, who chuckled again and ran a hand down my spine.

"Not the handsomest cat either," Akito said. He punctuated his comment with another uproarious laugh. His earring jangled over the loudspeaker.

I sniffed. Just shows what he knows. I get my fair share of admiration from felines of the feminine variety.

"Sort of a Rocky of the feline world," Akito continued. "You'll recognize him by the chunk missing from his ear, the bump on his nose, and the gash under one eye."

Those are scars of valor. I licked my paw with the missing nail and proudly rubbed the ear with its missing chunk. Any cat worth his whiskers sports a scar or two.

"Armed and dangerous."

I flexed my claws.

"Those claws leave quite a gouge. Ask any of us crew members." Akito burst into another explosive fit of laughter. His earring jangled furiously. "So don't pick him up if you see him," he advised. "Just call the nearest steward. Mrs. Clayton will be very grateful for his return and is offering a handsome reward to anyone who assists in locating him."

A reward? I sat straight up. Great balls of fur! I'd be bait for every fortune hunter on the entire ship, and from what I'd seen so far, this ship was full of them. I needed to find a better place to hide.

"A reward?" Alvin echoed my thoughts. He too sat straight up. "Everyone on the ship is going to be looking for you now, Inspector Paws. We'd better get you into Max's cabin pronto."

He grabbed a stack of towels from the cart, laid me on top of them, and stacked another pile of towels on top of me. I sneezed as the fluff from the towels tickled my nose. I'd never been part of a towel sandwich before. Not something I'd highly recommend, but if it got me safely to Stella's cabin, I could put up with a little discomfort.

We'd just turned the corner outside Garvey's suite when we ran into Max. She was dressed in Alvin's uniform and pushing a trolley loaded with rattling cups and saucers, a coffee urn, and two covered plates. The aroma of crispy bacon reminded me it had been far too long since my last meal.

"Hey!" Alvin grabbed Max's arm, nearly dumping me and the pile of towels onto the trolley. "Where are you going with that?" he demanded. "And what are you doing in my uniform? It's my shift, not yours."

Max grabbed for the coffee urn and steadied it on the tray.

"Watch it!" she cried. "You nearly spilled Garvey's coffee. And don't you go yelling at me." She slapped his arm away from the trolley. "You're the one that disappeared, aren't you? You didn't show up for your shift, so Akito called me. What did you expect me to do?"

Alvin lowered his head. "Well I'm here now, aren't I?" he mumbled. "I'll take over."

"Oh no you won't," Max said. "I'm on a mission now."

Alvin frowned. "What sort of mission?" he asked, his voice heavy with suspicion.

Max leaned toward him and lowered her voice to a conspiratorial whisper. "I've come up with a plan," she whispered.

Alvin eyed her warily, his frown deepening.

"What sort of plan?" he asked. "You're not going to get us into more trouble are you?"

Max flipped her head back and sniffed.

"Really, Alvin," she said. "You're such a scaredy cat!"

I yowled in protest. Who says cats are scared?

Max jumped and the trolley rattled beneath her hands.

"Is that Paws?" she asked.

Alvin squished me between the towels.

"Yes, it is," he answered. "But don't you go changing the subject. What's this new plan of yours?"

Max leaned across the trolley and grinned at Alvin.

"Listen," she said, once more lowering her voice to an excited whisper. "As soon as Aunt Jo and Gran disappeared for their excursion, I went in to Garvey's suite to make up the beds and clean the room. I thought Garvey would have gone to breakfast, but he and Angus Lloyd were both there. They were huddled over some papers, and Angus was begging Garvey to get Aunt Jo to sign them before tomorrow. As soon as I walked in, Angus stuffed the papers back into his briefcase as though they were stolen goods, and Garvey yelled at me that the beds could wait and I was to get him and Angus some breakfast."

Max paused, breathed in deeply, and grabbed the handles of the trolley.

"So here I am with their breakfast," she said.

She started to push the trolley toward Garvey's door, but Alvin stepped in front of it.

"Wait," he said. "You're not telling me everything, are you? What are you up to?"

"I'm going to find out what's in those papers, of course," Max said.

"And how do you think you're going to do that without getting caught?" Alvin asked.

"I'm pretty sure both Garvey and Angus will be taking a little nap soon," Max said. She smiled slyly and pulled the brim of her cap down lower on her head. "And once they're having that little nap, I'll just sneak back in and see what's in those papers."

"And just why would they be taking a nap?" Alvin asked, his eyes narrowing.

Max shrugged. "It could just be that I slipped a few of Gran's sleeping tablets into the urn of coffee," she said.

"You what?" Alvin leaned across the trolley.

"Shh," Max ordered. "Do you want them to hear you?"

Flapping whales' tails! What was she thinking? Stealing the papers was one thing, but dosing Garvey and Angus with sleeping pills? She could get in real trouble for that.

I squirmed out from between the towels, leaped into the middle of Max's trolley, and tumbled the whole tray onto the floor. Coffee splattered against the wall. Bacon and toast scattered around us. Cutlery clattered noisily against the metal trolley as it chased after the bits of bacon and toast.

"Inspector Paws!" Max shrieked.

The door to Garvey's room banged open, and Max's cry of dismay was drowned out by Garvey's bellow.

"Is that my breakfast?" he shouted.

Max cringed behind the trolley.

"Sorry, sir," she mumbled. "Bit of an accident. I'll get you another."

"Don't bother," Garvey said. Disgust dripped from each word as he watched egg drip off the edge of the trolley and onto the carpet of the corridor. "I'll go down to the cafeteria and get my own." He looked back into the room. "Come on, Angus. Let's get some breakfast."

"But sir." Angus scurried to the door and shoved some papers into Garvey's hand. "You've got to look at this contract first. It can't wait. It's got to be signed tonight. They're ready to start digging tomorrow. You know a delay could cost us a small fortune."

"Alright. Alright. Give me the papers," Garvey said. He snatched them out of Angus's hand. "And a pen. I'll sign them now."

He balanced the papers against the wall and scribbled his signature.

"There!" Garvey said. "I've signed them. I'll take Jo for a drink when she gets back from her little outing and get her to sign them. Happy?"

He waved the papers at Angus.

Great balls of fur! This was the contract they were trying to trick Jo into signing. This was all the ammunition we needed.

I didn't think twice. I leaped for the papers, grabbed them in my teeth, and took off. The papers slapped me in the face, while Garvey's bellow of rage chased me down the corridor.

# CHAPTER 14

It's no secret that the human kind idolize love. They chase after it the same way I chase after a bird, fascinated by its tweets and twitters. Why else would Jo be so eager to enter into marriage number four? But I never thought they'd go so far as to build a shrine to it. Each letter stood at least five feet tall. They were twined together in an artistic display mounted on the wall behind the head table. L-O-V-E.

The entire room whispered love and romance, from the creamy damask tablecloths to the crystal hearts dangling from the ceiling and casting rainbows of candlelight on the tables below. Red roses, white candles, and delicate baby's breath adorned each table. A giant engagement ring and matching wedding band, both carved of ice, encircled each other atop a bed of roses in the center of the head table. The rings sparkled in the setting sun as though created from the very diamonds they represented. It was indeed a perfect setting for a rehearsal dinner. Too bad I'd have to spoil it.

I jumped onto the table. The L-O-V-E sign would be a perfect hiding spot and give me a birds-eye view of all who entered. I leaped toward the shelf that formed part of the L, but my feet slipped on the silky tablecloth. Crystal stemware toppled against each other in a tinkling symphony. Plates slid to the edge of the table and held on for dear life. A silver fork tumbled over the edge and pinged to the floor. I dug my claws into the rim of the L and slowly pulled myself onto the ledge. Tucking the wad of paper firmly beneath me, I stretched out to wait for Jo.

This hadn't been my original plan. After stealing the papers, I'd scrunched them into a tight wad so they were easier to carry. I'd hidden most of the day by the gangplank waiting for Jo and Stella to return from their excursion to Skagway.

There was no missing them when they finally arrived. Their tightly fitted matching red dresses with the ruffled necklines that showed more skin than sense, their feathered hats, their black diamond-patterned sheer stockings with the line up the middle of their calves set them well apart from the rest of the crowd as they hobbled onto the ship in their spiky red shoes.

Miriam Turner appeared behind them.

"Really," she said, her lip curling in derision. "Some people will wear anything."

Jo lifted her nose in the air. The feather in her hat waved wildly back and forth.

"And I say one should always dress the part," Jo sniffed.

"Just because you're visiting a brothel, doesn't mean you have to dress like a tart, Mrs. Bellamy," Miriam replied. "I'm surprised that fiancé of yours lets you dress like that."

"My fiancé doesn't tell me how to dress," Jo said.

Miriam's eyebrows rose. "Really?" she said. "Perhaps not yet, but he will, you know."

"He will not," Jo said. "Unlike you, Leroy delights in my uniqueness. He allows me to be myself."

Miriam smiled thinly. "You don't know him very well, do you, Mrs. Bellamy?"

Not waiting for a reply, she squeezed past Jo and Stella trying to avoid any contact with their outlandish costumes.

"Well, of all the nerve!" Jo muttered. She shook herself as though trying to shake off Miriam's comments. The feather in her hat waved back and forth as though mocking Miriam's stiff back.

"Never mind her," Stella said. "Some people are just born uptight." She gave Jo a quick hug, and then pulled her close to her. "But she could be right about Leroy, you know," she added. "It's not too late to back out of this marriage, you know. Wait until you know him better."

Jo pulled away from Stella. Her eyes blazed fire.

"I know everything I need to know about Leroy," Jo said. "And I intend to marry him whether you like him or not."

"But even you have to admit he has a terrible temper," Stella said.

"And that's because of you," Jo said. "It's obvious to everyone that you don't like him. That's enough to put anyone on edge. And then you bring Paws along. Paws is driving Leroy absolutely mad."

Me? Shiver me whiskers! The man was mad long before he'd ever met me. I pulled myself up to my full height. I wasn't about to lie here and take that. I'd just toss this contract at Jo's feet and then we'd see what she thought of her beloved Garvey.

I grabbed the wad of paper in my mouth and started to slide out from under the bench I'd been hiding under, when Garvey's booming voice stopped me.

"Hello, Ladies," Garvey said. His good will seemed a little forced. "How was Skagway?"

I quickly slid back into my hiding place. If I dropped the contract at Jo's feet now, Garvey would just grab it and destroy it.

Garvey apparently noticed the vibe of friction between Jo and Stella.

"Anything wrong, ladies?" he asked.

Jo shook off her anger and smiled at him. "Not a thing, my dear. Just having a little discussion, that's all." She tried to hustle him away, but he turned to Stella.

"Found that cat of yours yet, Stella?" he asked.

A sudden look of concern appeared on Stella's face.

"No, I haven't," she said. "And I'm so worried."

What a load of dirty cat litter! If she'd been worried about me, she wouldn't have been gallivanting in Skagway's brothels, would she?

"Think I'll just pop in to see if the captain's had any luck," she said.

I swallowed the growl forming in my throat. How dare she use me as an excuse to visit the captain? I would have given away my whereabouts if Garvey hadn't chosen that moment to issue his accusation.

"Your cat stole some papers from me," Garvey said.

"Papers?" A sparkle of excitement lit up Stella's eyes. "I do hope they weren't important."

"Not so much important as confidential," Leroy said. "If you find them, don't read them. Either shred them or get them back to me."

He took Jo's arm and led her away.

I tucked the wad of papers more securely under my stomach. How was I going to get them to Jo without Garvey snatching them away? I thought about giving them to Stella. She hadn't looked like she'd obey Garvey's instructions and just shred them, but she'd probably show them to the captain and the captain, of course, would insist on doing the right thing and returning them to Garvey. Somehow I had to give them directly to Jo.

I trotted up the stairs to the very top deck of the ship, the wad of paper dangling awkwardly from my mouth, and slipped into Neptune's Loft. This was the private dining room with a panoramic view of the ocean where the rehearsal dinner was to be held. All I had to do was wait for Jo and hope Leroy and Angus hadn't already conned her into signing a duplicate of this contract.

I nuzzled the wad of papers with my nose. It was still safely tucked underneath me. Now all I needed was to have that fickle feline luck smile upon me and send Jo in early. Maybe she'd come in to check everything was set up okay. But, of course, lady luck was being her usual fickle self. It was Patricia Garvey who arrived first.

She stood in the doorway as though hesitant to enter.

"Go on." Miriam Turner's voice came from just outside the door.

What was Miriam Turner doing here? Surely she hadn't been invited to the rehearsal dinner.

"You've every right to make your own decisions," Miriam said.

She must have given Patricia a shove, because Patricia stumbled awkwardly into the room. Tyler Onslow, looking every bit the impish angel in his white tuxedo with golden buttons and his halo of curly hair, followed close on her heels.

Great balls of fur! I wasn't the only one about to ruin this dinner. One sight of Tyler with Patricia, and Garvey would be off on one of his tantrums.

Tyler led Patricia to a spot as far away from the head table as possible and pulled out a chair for her, but Patricia seemed reluctant to sit down.

"Oh, Tyler, do you really think this is a good idea?" she asked.

"Of course it is." Tyler shoved the chair into the back of her knees, and she was forced to sit. "Mrs. Turner is right. You need to assert yourself. You're over eighteen, and he can't tell you who you can and can't see."

Stella's trilling laugh brought my attention back to the doorway. I was hoping she'd have Jo with her, but no such luck. Captain Bonar was at her side, and she was looking up at him with that look that belonged to Ernie. A growl formed in the pit of my belly, but I forced it back down. If I revealed myself now, there'd be no way of getting this contract safely into Jo's hands. The issue of Stella and the captain would have to wait.

Stella stumbled in the doorway. Served her right for trying to hobble around on stilts. She grabbed for the captain's arm. I should have known it was just a ruse to grab hold of him. Her purse slid off her shoulder and the contents spread over the floor.

"Trust me to make an entrance," Stella said. She giggled up at the captain, her eyes flirting with his.

Captain Bonar gallantly collected her bag and stuffed the belongings back in. He didn't notice the notepad that had dropped behind him, but Miriam Turner did. She picked it up. Her lip curled derisively as she looked at it. She tapped Stella on the shoulder, and held the notepad out to her. The notepad dangled between her thumb and one finger as though she could hardly bare to touch it.

"I believe this is yours, Mrs. Clayton," she said.

"Oh, my notepad!" Stella grabbed for it, her eyes lighting up with excitement. "I found that in Skagway. Isn't it darling? I'd have been so sorry to lose that."

"Of course." Miriam's voice dripped with sarcasm. "One would be totally lost without a notepad showing a cat riding on the back of a polar bear and reading *having a purrfectly roaring time.*"

"He looks so much like Paws," Stella said. She either hadn't heard the sarcasm in Miriam's voice or chose to ignore it. "Don't you think so, Gideon?" she asked. She handed the notepad to the captain.

The captain looked at it, raised an eyebrow, and handed it back to Stella.

"Might look more like Inspector Paws if he were running in front of a dogsled," he said. He laughed heartily at his unfeeling witticism.

Bad enough that he'd dragged me on that dogsled excursion, but to make fun of me for it, that was more than any cat should have to endure. The growl once more formed in my throat, and I had to stuff it back down.

A brief look of concern flitted across Stella's face. "I do wonder where he is," she said. "Has no one seen him, Gideon?"

"Oh yes, he's been seen," the captain replied. "Catching him is another matter. Like I said, no need to worry about Inspector Paws. He's one canny cat. He'll show up. The question is when, and where, and at who's expense?"

"If you ask me," Miriam Turner said. She tossed her nose in the air as though trying to escape a bad smell. "The world would be a whole lot better if both that cat and that notepad were sent adrift on an iceberg."

I could tell by the look she gave Stella that she wanted to lump her in with the undesirables as well, but didn't quite have the nerve.

Captain Bonar put a protective arm around Stella.

"What an unkind remark, Miriam," he said. "By the way, what are you doing here? Surely you haven't been invited to the rehearsal dinner."

"Of course not," Miriam replied. "And I wouldn't attend even if I had been. I was just here to give Patricia a little encouragement."

"Encouragement?" the captain asked. He eyed Miriam warily.

A brief smile flitted across Miriam's face. "Patricia seemed a little hesitant to bring Tyler as her escort," she said. She tossed her head and marched away.

"She brought Tyler?" Stella questioned. She sounded genuinely concerned, though why she should worry about Garvey going into another tantrum was more than I could fathom. Wasn't that what she wanted? To show Jo what Garvey was made of?

Tyler waved at them from across the room. He whispered something in Patricia's ear. Patricia smiled and looked up somewhat fearfully.

I was distracted from any further actions of Patricia and Tyler by the heavenly smell of shrimp. I breathed in deeply and looked around to see where the aroma was coming from. Max entered from the door at the back of the room. She was dressed in Alvin's costume and carrying a tray of shrimp cocktail.

Lorne Akito followed her in. Even dressed in a sober black tuxedo, he resembled a pirate. His gold earring sparkled in the setting sun, and his teeth gleamed whitely as he grinned at Max.

"Just put one of those in the center of each place setting," he said. "Think you can handle it?"

Max tossed her head in annoyance. In normal circumstances, her long, red ponytail would have smacked him in the face, but it was firmly tucked into Alvin's ball cap.

"I can handle any ..." Her words froze as she looked toward the doorway and spotted Stella and the captain. One of the cocktails slid across her tray and would have landed on the carpet if Lorne's hand hadn't darted out and caught it.

Captain Bonar stiffened. His eyes widened. In less time than it took for me to turn my head, he was standing beside Max.

"You're not Alvin," the captain said.

The dishes of shrimp cocktail rattled on Max's tray as she trembled under the captain's harsh voice. For once she had nothing to say.

The captain's eyes swept over to the corner where the Pirates of Georgia Straight were tuning their instruments.

"So I suppose," he said thoughtfully. "Max Clayton, the young guitar player who's wowing everyone with her talents, is actually Alvin." He looked down at Max. Max nodded, then took a deep breath as though she were about to say something, but the captain looked at Akito instead.

"And you knew about this?" Captain Bonar asked.

"I can explain, sir," Akito said. For once his head didn't bobble, and his earring was silent.

Stella interrupted by grabbing the captain's arm.

"Let him explain later, Gideon," she said. "This isn't the time or place. Jo and Leroy will be arriving any minute. Let's go find our seats."

Captain Bonar gave Akito and Max another withering glance before letting Stella drag him to the head table.

They sat directly below me. Stella had her back to me, but the captain was seated on her right at the head of the table. All he had to do was look up and he'd be staring me in the eye. I held my breath, not daring to move a whisker. If only Jo would hurry up and make her appearance before the captain saw me.

As though sensing my urgency, Jo suddenly appeared in the doorway. She was dressed for the part, as she no doubt would have put it. Not exactly a fairy princess — she was much too old for that — but dressed totally in white, she did look like she might have stepped out of some fairytale or one of those Victorian movies that Stella liked to watch. Her white, crocheted gown rippled as she walked. The wide brim of her hat flopped gracefully, sending tantalizing shadows flitting across her face. A white chiffon scarf, draped loosely around the brim of her hat, flowed out behind her as though she were walking in a dream.

The dream turned to a nightmare as Garvey took his place on one side of Jo and Angus on the other like bodyguards.

Great balls of fur! How could I possibly get the paper to Jo without one of those two grabbing it first?

Everyone stood as the wedding couple entered, and I was eye-to-eye with Captain Bonar. The captain drew a sharp breath and touched Stella's shoulder.

"Look," he whispered.

Stella's head swiveled around, and she stared up at me. Her face lit up.

"Paws!"

The captain's hand clamped over her mouth before she could say anything more.

"Leave him," the captain whispered. "Garvey has enough unwanted guests at his party. We know where he is. I'll get him later."

Not if I had anything to say about it. I sank back down onto my ledge with a sigh of relief. I was safe, at least for the time being. I just had to wait for the right time to drop this paper in Jo's lap.

Jo and Garvey took their places behind the intertwined ice rings. Angus sat at the end of the table opposite to Captain Bonar. An empty chair remained beside Garvey. Garvey frowned at the empty chair, and then looked around the room.

"Where's Patricia?" he asked.

"I'm here, Daddy." Patricia waved at him from her place beside Tyler. Red splotches appeared in each of her cheeks.

Garvey's knuckles turned white as he gripped the back of

his chair. The color rose in his face like a volcano about to explode.

"You!" His eyes bored into Tyler. "What are you doing here?"

Tyler merely raised an eyebrow and grinned his angelic grin.

"Your daughter invited me, sir," he replied.

"Out!" Garvey jabbed a finger at Tyler, and then pointed to the door.

"Okay. Okay." Tyler held up his hands in surrender and turned to leave, but Patricia grabbed his arm and held him back. The color in Patricia's face rose, and so did her voice.

"He's my guest, father. You've no right to throw him out."

"Of course he has a right, Patti," Tyler said. "It's his party. Never mind, we'll work it out later." He gently tugged himself free.

"We'll work it out now," Patricia said. Some of her father's stubbornness had seeped into her voice. "I'll choose my own friends, Daddy," she said. "I'm over eighteen. You have no right to tell me who and who I can't have for friends."

"That sounds like a quote from Miriam Turner," Garvey bellowed.

"What if it is?" Patricia yelled back. "It's true. And if Tyler's not welcome here, then I'm leaving too." She headed for the door.

"Patricia, wait!" Garvey ordered. He tried to grab her arm to prevent her leaving, but she tugged herself free. "I only want what's best for you," he pleaded. "That boy's a fortune hunter. He'll just lure you into a life of heartache and pain!"

A loud thump of a discordant guitar drew everyone's attention to the corner where the band had set up. Alvin shoved past the bass player. His face under the red bandana was twisted into a grimace of pain and anger. He waved his guitar in Garvey's direction.

"Just like you did to my mother!" he yelled, and then raced out of the room.

Captain Bonar shoved back his chair and was about to follow Alvin out, but Garvey's booming bellow stopped him.

"And where do you think you're going, Captain Bonar?" he yelled. "You'll pay for that. You'll pay for this whole bloody mess! You can't even control your son. How do you think you can captain a ship?"

Jo put a hand on Garvey's arm and tried to calm him down, but he shrugged free of her.

"You'll hear from my lawyers, Captain," he continued. "I'm suing you — you and your entire cruise line — for that disastrous excursion, for assault, and now for ruining my rehearsal dinner." He stopped to gulp in some air before continuing. "I'm going to sue for breach of contract."

Contract? I'd been so caught up in the fracas, I'd nearly forgotten. This was as good a time as any to drop the contract on Jo's plate.

I jumped to the center of the table. Dishes rattled. Stella and Jo shrieked. The ice rings tottered on the centerpiece but miraculously stayed in place. I dropped my wad of paper on Jo's plate.

Angus grabbed for it, but Jo was quicker.

"What's this?" she asked. She tried to smooth out the scrunched pages. "This is a contract to allow digging on the Ravens Island property." Her eyes flew to Leroy. "But that's my property."

"It's nothing, Jo," Leroy said.

His anger seemed to have suddenly evaporated. He smiled

and tried to put an arm around Jo, but Jo backed away from him, and flipped to the last page. She stared at Leroy's signature.

"Nothing?" she asked. "That's why you're marrying me, isn't it? You think I'll sign this contract now that we're to be married?" Her voice rose with each question. "I refused to sign this contract because that land harbors a wild life habitat. I refused to sign for conservation reasons. Do you really think marrying you would change my mind?"

"Jo! Jo! Calm down." Garvey reached for her hand, but Jo pulled away. "It's just a draft — an old draft," he pleaded, "Can't imagine where the cat dug it up from."

Jo jabbed a finger at the bottom of the crumpled page.

"A draft? Signed by you? No one signs a draft. And it's dated today. Do you think I'm a fool?"

"That's just a random date. Tell her, Angus."

Jo scrunched the paper into a ball, chucked it at Garvey, and headed for the door.

"Random or not, the wedding's off!"

She yanked the large engagement ring off her finger and flung it at Garvey. It bounced off his glasses and landed in his shrimp cocktail, the juice splattering his tuxedo.

Jo sailed out the door. The wind grabbed her floppy hat and tossed it out to sea. Her white chiffon scarf caught on the railing and flapped wildly.

Garvey sank into his chair and buried his head in his hands.

"Everyone out!" he ordered.

I wasted no time obeying and raced for the doorway, neck and neck with Lorne Akito.

"Not you," Garvey bellowed.

I slid under the nearest table at the sound of his voice, and Lorne skidded to a stop.

"Get me a large bottle of scotch. Better make it two," Garvey said.

Lorne hurried off, along with everyone else in the room. Only Angus Lloyd remained. He hovered at the end of Garvey's table.

"Shall I stay, sir?" Angus asked.

"No." Garvey shook his head. He fished Jo's engagement ring out of his shrimp cocktail, studied it carefully, and then lifted his arm as though to throw it out the open window.

Angus reached for it. "I'll take that, shall I?" he asked. "It's still returnable."

Garvey laughed, a hoarse, ragged laugh that grated the spine. He handed the ring to Angus.

"Money," he said. "That's all you think about, Angus, isn't it?"

CHAPTER 15

I EXPECTED AT LEAST a smidgeon of gratitude from Stella and Max when I trotted up to their cabin and scratched on the door to be let in. Hadn't I almost single-handedly stopped Jo from marrying the dreadful Garvey? Isn't that what they'd wanted? I knew better than to expect to be hailed as a conquering hero. Neither one of them would want to admit I'd done it without their help. But I did expect a few kisses, a word of thanks, perhaps a celebratory feast.

Instead they didn't seem the least bit pleased to see me.

"Oh, Paws," Stella chided, as she opened the door and dragged me inside. "What a fracas you've caused."

She held her cell phone pressed to her ear for several minutes, then closed it and dropped it into her tote bag with a worried frown.

"Oh, where or where could Jo be?" she muttered.

She paced the room for a while and then headed for the door.

"I'm going out to look for her," she said. She turned at the door and shook a finger at me. "You stay here," she ordered. "And don't get into any more mischief."

Great shivering whiskers! What had I done to deserve this kind of treatment? I sprawled on the floor and licked angrily at my outstretched paws.

Max was no better. She nearly tripped over me in her haste to catch up with Stella.

"Wait, Gran," she shouted. "I'll come with you. Maybe we can find Alvin, too."

She swung the door wide and let it close on its own, but not before I slipped through and into the hallway.

If that's how they felt, I'd find somewhere else to spend the rest of this abominable cruise, somewhere where I was appreciated. Maybe that impish angel, Tyler, would take me in. Or even Alvin. Alvin hadn't seemed to mind my company, and I had a good idea where he was hiding.

I trotted down to the pool deck. A cold wind ruffled the fur on my neck. I shivered. The storm the captain had predicted had taken over the whole ship now, both inside and out. Billowing black clouds whirled and swirled above me in a dark and deadly dance. I dared a quick peek at the ocean. The white caps, as though mesmerized by the swirling dark clouds, rose angrily out of the sea, lapping and tugging at the sides of the boat, trying to pull it under. The boat rolled to the right, and I slid helplessly across the deck. I clawed frantically at the deck's carpeting to keep from falling into the pool. Another roll of the ship sent me skittering towards the railing. Perhaps the pool deck wasn't the safest hiding place after all. I glanced over towards the towel rack Alvin and I had hidden behind last night. It swayed dangerously in a gust of wind. A towel tumbled to the deck.

I hurried past the bar and into the relative safety of the Sea Nymphs Cafeteria. At least here there were walls to keep me from falling into the sea. Dishes rattled as I entered. The boat rolled, and I slid under one of the tables. I clawed my way back to the center aisle and looked around. It had been a long time since I'd had a decent meal. Perhaps a midnight snack was in order. But all the best dishes had been packed away. What remained was a smattering of snack foods and deserts.

I remembered the shrimp cocktail that Max had set out at the rehearsal dinner. Would they still be there lined up on the tables in Neptune's Loft? It was past midnight. Surely Garvey would have left by now. Even if he hadn't, with two bottles of scotch in him, he'd hardly notice one tiny cat nibbling a few shrimp. If Stella and Max wouldn't treat me to a celebratory feast, I'd have one all by myself.

I scampered up the stairs to Neptune's Loft. The door was firmly shut. Even my desperate clawing couldn't move it. My stomach rumbled in disappointment. I could try the windows. They'd been open earlier. But to get to them I'd have to crawl along the railing.

The boat tilted, and I slid across the deck, crashing into the glass partition below the railing. Did I dare climb onto that railing and try to balance myself in this wind? Visions of savory pink shrimp flashed before my eyes. Some things are worth the risk.

I clamored onto the railing, scurried along it as quickly and carefully as I could, and found myself under an open window. I placed my front paws on the windowsill and peered into the room.

There was no sign of Garvey. One full bottle of scotch and another half empty one stood beside his empty glass marking the spot where he'd sat. Another barely touched glass of scotch sat across the table. Garvey must have had company. And from the looks of the upended chair, whoever he'd been sharing a drink with had left in a hurry. Garvey's chair seemed to have disappeared as well. Perhaps they'd both left in a hurry.

No matter. The shrimp cocktails were still there, all lined up waiting for a hungry cat.

A gust of wind gave me a shove, and I leaped through the window and onto the head table. The table shook. Dishes rattled. I looked over to see if the ice rings had toppled, but they weren't there.

I peered over the edge of the table, and all thought of tasty shrimp deserted me.

Leroy Garvey sprawled lifeless on the floor in a pool of blood. One of the ice rings circled his head like an ice cap. The other lay shattered on his chest. An icy shard pierced his eye. It was the same eye Jo's engagement ring would have hit earlier if he hadn't been wearing his glasses. Perhaps if he'd worn his glasses this time, he'd still be alive, but he'd removed them. They were now firmly clutched in his left hand.

Something white and silky lifted from under him and flapped in the breeze from the open window. The fur on the back of my neck rose. Was that his spirit rising from beneath him? I shook the nonsense out of myself. Garvey's spirit would be anything but light and silky.

I jumped to the floor for a closer look.

Garvey's dead hand throttled Jo's scarf, the one that had graced her floppy hat earlier in the evening, the one that had flown off when she stomped out of the room, the one I'd last seen caught on the railing, flapping like a warning flag. Now it lay firmly tucked under Garvey's head, one end blood-soaked and soggy, the other end rising and falling in the breeze.

Cat-o-Nine-Tails! Had my meddling pushed Jo to murder? Had she come back for her scarf, come in here, and killed Garvey?

Lorne Akito's booming voice made me jump. He was just outside the door.

"I've got to get those ice rings, and you're coming with me," he ordered.

"But I've got to go, Lorne." Max's voice rose in protest. "Gran will be frantic if I don't get back there."

Flapping whales' tales! They'd be in here any minute. I couldn't let them find Jo's scarf under Garvey's skull, flapping away, telling everyone what she'd done. Since I'd driven her to it, it was up to me to get her out of this mess. I'd have to remove the evidence. I grabbed the end of Jo's scarf in my mouth and tugged, but it stuck firmly under Garvey's head.

The door knob rattled again.

"Listen to me, young lady. You've caused me enough trouble." There was no laughter in Lorne's voice now. "I need those rings. Who knows? With those two, the wedding could be on again tomorrow, and it would be more than my life's worth if those rings aren't front and center. But I'm not going in there alone, not with an angry Garvey brooding in there."

"You want me for protection," Max scoffed.

"I want you for a witness should anything happen," Lorne said. "Now move it, young lady."

"Fine," Max said. "Let's get it over with."

The door burst open. A trolley rattled across the floor. I gave another desperate tug. Garvey's hand moved but refused to let go of the silky scarf.

"Anyway," Max said. "I didn't get you in trouble. You were just as pleased as Alvin and me about the switch."

That was one of Max's most annoying traits. She never knew when to leave well enough alone. She always had to get in the last word.

"Alvin was the best thing that happened to that pirate band of yours," Max added.

"Are you always this mouthy?" Akito asked.

I could have told him this was mild.

Max gave a laugh laced with a large dose of scorn. "Really, Lorne," she scoffed. "All that fear and Garvey isn't even in here."

Akito was silent for a minute, and then gave a sheepish laugh of his own.

"But since you're here," he said. "You might as well help me load the rings onto the trolley."

"But the rings are gone," Max said.

"Gone?" Akito sounded worried. "Gone where?"

The rattling trolley sped toward the table. They'd be onto me in a minute. I braced my legs and yanked. The scarf pulled free. Garvey's hand thudded back onto the floor.

"What was that?" Max asked.

Both Lorne and Max peered over the edge of the table. Their eyes widened. They screamed in unison.

I stood paralyzed as the blood-soaked scarf flapped wildly in my mouth.

"Inspector Paws! What have you done?" Max shrieked.

Me? Did she think I'd killed Garvey?

Max dived for me, but I dodged out of her way.

"Call the captain," she ordered.

Lorne pried his fingers off the handles of the trolley and slowly fumbled his cell phone out of his pocket.

I dropped the end of the scarf and ran.

Max grabbed an ice bucket off the table, and with the accuracy of a skilled basketball player, heaved it at me. The bucket descended over my head. Its walls surrounded me, blocking out the last of the light. Chunks of melting ice tumbled over my shaking body and froze me in place.

Max stomped a foot on top of the bucket.

I was trapped. Ice water seeped into the fur of my neck. Is this how Garvey had felt, I wondered. Had he died instantly, or had the chill of the melting ice rings seeped into his bones and sent his body into uncontrollable fits of shivering?

"Captain," Lorne said into his cell phone. His voice trembled almost as much as his earring. "There's been a murder, sir. In Neptune's Loft."

CHAPTER 16

MY SHIVERING WAS ALMOST under control by the time the captain hauled me back to his quarters and tossed me into the brig, but I took one look out of that huge window with its panoramic view of the ocean, and the shakes began all over again. The waves, which had been mere ripples a few days before, had worked themselves into a frenzy. The entire sea bubbled like a giant cauldron boiling out of control. White spray shot high into the air with each gust of wind, shrouding the rising sun in a curtain of steamy mist. The sun struggled valiantly to break through the haze, but only managed to cut an eerie red path across the bubbling waves as though lighting them on fire.

"What a fine mess this is," Captain Bonar muttered. He paced back and forth.

You'd think he was the one locked in the brig.

The boat tilted, and I slid helplessly across the cage, my nose bumping into the metal grid of bars. Captain Bonar grabbed the stair railing to steady himself, and then picked up the bar stool that had skidded into his shins as though nothing was wrong.

Shiver me whiskers! What was the man still doing here? Shouldn't he be up on the bridge making sure this ship didn't flip over and dump us all into that angry sea?

I licked furiously at my fur, trying to get my nerves under

control, and then scanned the inside of my cage. There had to be a way out of here. If this boat was going down, I didn't want to be locked in this jewelry display case, perfectly wrapped and packaged for Davey Jones locker.

The captain pulled out his cell phone and punched in a number.

"Where's that report?" he barked.

Almost before he'd shoved the phone back into his pocket, Paul Marco, the staff captain, entered the room. He was shorter than the captain, but stood stiff and erect as though that would increase his height. Even when the boat swayed and I once more slid across the cage, the staff captain stood stiff and erect. Perhaps his starchy white uniform was holding him up.

"Everything's under control, sir," he said, his voice as stiff and crisp as his uniform. "We've arrested Jo Bellamy. It's pretty obvious she killed him."

"It was Jo then?" the captain asked. "And not the cat?"

Cat-o-Nine-Tails! Was he trying to pin this murder on me? I yowled my objection, but neither one of them paid any attention. Surely anyone with half a brain would know I couldn't toss those ice rings at a fully grown man, not unless he was already sprawled on the floor, and with only a finger of scotch gone from the bottle, there was little chance Garvey had drunk himself into that state.

"Oh, no, sir," Marco said. He shook his head stiffly. "There's no way the cat could have thrown those ice rings at Garvey's head."

Captain Bonar sighed.

Was that a sigh of relief or disappointment? It was difficult to tell.

"And you're sure it was Jo Bellamy?" the captain asked.

"Of course, sir," Marco replied, sounding slightly annoyed

that the captain should question his judgment. "It was her scarf under the deceased's body. She'd had quite a row with him earlier. Everyone at the dinner agrees on that. And she can't account for her whereabouts at the time of his death."

"Where is she now?" the captain asked.

"We locked her in that empty cabin just down the hall from here. Inside cabin, you know. Don't want her jumping ship, do we?"

"How's she taking it?" the captain asked, sounding a little apprehensive.

"Kicking up quite a fuss at the moment, sir. Yelling like a banshee."

Well, of course she'd be yelling. Being locked in a room, no matter how big, drove Jo to a state of sheer madness. She'd been locked in her garage one time when the door opener jammed. Her screams had brought the whole neighborhood running. Ernie managed to pry the door open, and Jo burst out in such a frenzy, swinging a crowbar over her head, that Ernie had to run for cover.

"She's crazy! Absolutely, crazy!" Ernie had said to Stella. "I don't want you hanging out with her anymore."

But Stella had defended Jo. "Nonsense," she said. "Jo's not crazy, just a bit eccentric. And she's claustrophobic. Claustrophobia makes people do strange things."

There's no telling what Jo might do locked in that room down the hall.

If it hadn't been for me she wouldn't have found out about Garvey's little scheme; she wouldn't have been driven to murder him; and she wouldn't be locked in that little room. Somehow I had to get her out of there.

But was it really Jo who'd killed Garvey? A picture of the practically untouched glass of scotch flashed into my brain. Jo didn't drink scotch. It must have been someone else sitting at the table across from Garvey. Who was it? All the more reason for me to get free of this cage. I had to find answers. I attacked the hinge of my cage with renewed vigor.

"And you've dealt with the body?" the captain asked.

He paced across the floor, stared out the window, and then paced back to where Marco stood by the door, stiff as a starched sentinel.

"Of course, sir," Marco replied. There was no missing the tone of offence in his voice. "We took pictures before removing the body. We've sealed up the room pending investigation by the Vancouver authorities when we get back to port. The room was remarkably undisturbed, sir. I suppose because the dinner party never really got underway. We did find this button."

He held up a button enclosed in a plastic package.

I stopped clawing at the bars and peered through them for a closer look. It was a shiny gold button. Where had I seen one like that before?

"Where'd you find it?" Captain Bonar asked.

"Just under the window."

"And nothing else?"

"Nothing else." Marco hesitated, frowned, and then cleared his throat, but whatever he was about to say was drowned out by Stella's high-pitched shout just outside the door.

"Gideon! Gideon!" Stella shouted, banging on the door.

Captain Bonar hurried to let her in. She and Max both tumbled into the room, nearly knocking Marco off balance. He quickly backed against the wall and clung to it as though his life depended on it. His eyes darted fearfully from one to the other. I couldn't really blame him for being a little startled. Max and Stella, both jabbering at the same time, were enough to give even the stiffest and starchiest of men the shakes.

"They've arrested Jo. You've got to do something," Stella said. She tugged on the captain's arm and tried to drag him out the door.

Max grabbed his other arm. Her flailing red ponytail slapped Marco in the face. He inched closer to the wall.

"You can't go around locking people up just because you think they did something, Captain," Max declared. She caught sight of me, flung the captain's arm away, and raced over to my cage, her red ponytail flying behind her. "Or cats either," she shouted.

She bent close to the cage. "Don't you worry, Inspector Paws," she said. "I'll get you out of here."

I closed my eyes and pretended to ignore her. I wasn't fool enough to count on Max to get me out of here. She was the one who'd gotten me in here in the first place.

"Now, look here." Staff Captain Marco's voice cut across the room like the sword of a swashbuckling pirate.

Even Max jumped. She spun to face him, her flailing ponytail slapping against the bars of my cage.

The staff captain appeared to have recovered his nerve. He pushed himself away from the wall, planted himself in the middle of the room, and glared at both Stella and Max.

"If you're referring to Mrs. Bellamy," he said, his voice once more starched and clipped. "We've done a very thorough investigation, and we have no doubt at all that she killed her fiancé. She'll remain in custody until we hand her over to the proper authorities in Vancouver."

"But she didn't do it," Stella protested.

"And what happened to innocent until proven guilty?" Max demanded. She tossed her ponytail defiantly and made a step towards Marco, but the boat tilted and she slid across the floor, bumping into Stella. They both would have fallen if Captain

Bonar hadn't caught them. He threw an arm around each of them and tried to usher them toward the sofa.

"It's okay," he said. His voice softened. "Come and sit down."

"Sit down?" Stella's voice rose hysterically, and she pulled away from the captain's embrace. "I won't sit down. Not with Jo locked in that cabin."

Max too pulled away from the captain. "She's claustrophobic, you know," she said. Her voice rose in anger, and she punched the captain's shoulder. "She can't stand enclosed spaces. You've got to let her out."

"I'm afraid we can't do that," Captain Bonar replied. His voice remained calm and filled with concern. He rubbed his arm and stared at Stella, his eyes pleading with her for understanding.

"But she didn't do it," Stella said. She clasped her hands in front of her and gazed earnestly at the captain as though he were some god who could grant her every wish. "I know Jo didn't kill Garvey," she said. "She was with me the whole time. When she left the rehearsal dinner, she went to my room. She was sitting on the floor outside my door when I got back. I was with her the whole time."

I stopped pawing at the bars and stared at Stella. She was lying. Jo wasn't in her room when I got there. Didn't Stella know lying would only get her into more trouble?

"Now, really, Mrs. Clayton," Marco interrupted, his voice full of disbelief. "Lying ..."

Captain Bonar raised a hand, and Marco's words cut off mid-flow. The captain looked at Max.

"Is this true, Max?" he asked. "Was Mrs. Bellamy in your room all night?"

Max shuffled her feet. "I was late getting in," she muttered. She screwed up her face and looked over at Stella. "Oh, Gran, I can't lie. And it won't help Aunt Jo anyway if we lie. She wasn't there when I got to the room."

Stella glared at Max. "She'd just gone back to her room to pack some things. She was going to move in with us until we got back to Vancouver."

Marco sniffed in derision. "My dear Mrs. Clayton," he said. "The evidence against your friend is overwhelming."

Cat-o-Nine-Tails! Lying to protect Jo could get Stella into almost as much trouble as Jo. They could both go to prison, and what would become of me then? I clawed furiously at the trembling hinge. I had to get out of here and find out if Jo really was innocent, and if she was, who did kill Leroy Garvey?

The boat tilted roughly, and I slid across the cage. Stella tottered against Captain Bonar, who stole the opportunity to put a protective arm around her and guide her to a chair. Max skidded across the floor and smacked into Paul Marco, who stood firmly in place as though the boat hadn't moved at all. Max grabbed Marco's arms to steady herself and stared up at him challengingly.

"Just because I didn't see Aunt Jo with Gran, doesn't mean it's not true," Max said. "And besides, there are lots of other people who could have killed Garvey."

Paul Marco looked down his nose at Max's angry face.

"As I told you," he said. "All of the evidence points to Mrs. Bellamy."

"What about that extra glass of scotch on the table?" Max demanded. "He shared his bottle of scotch with someone, and it certainly wasn't Aunt Jo. Aunt Jo hates scotch."

"And how would you know about the extra glass?" Marco scowled down at her. "That room is sealed off."

Max flipped her red ponytail and glared up at him defiantly.

"Because I was there, wasn't I? I was the one that found the body."

"I knew it!" Stella said, excitement returning to her voice. She jumped up from the chair the captain had ushered her to, raced across the room, and grabbed Marco's starched arm. Marco's eyebrows rose in terror, but he held his ground.

"I knew someone else must have done it," Stella said. She hugged Max, and the two of them jumped up and down excitedly. "All we have do," Stella said. "Is find out who that visitor was."

Captain Bonar put a restraining hand on Stella's shoulder.

"But Stella," he said. "The scarf proves that Jo returned. We both saw that scarf fly off her hat when she left the room. She must have come back, retrieved it, and gone in to talk to Garvey. Maybe it was self defense, Stella. We'll get her a good lawyer."

Stella yanked herself free of the captain's hold. The captain stumbled into Paul Marco, nearly knocking him off his feet.

"She didn't do it, I tell you!" Stella shouted.

"Be reasonable, Stella," the captain pleaded, regaining his foothold. "How else did her scarf get there?"

"Someone tried to frame her," Stella said.

"The visitor tried to frame Aunt Jo," Max said, her voice filled with excitement. "We need to find out who was drinking that glass of scotch with Garvey."

Captain Bonar frowned and turned a questioning look on Marco.

"What about that glass, Marco?" he asked.

A hint of doubt crept into Marco's eyes. "I thought it was Mrs. Bellamy's," he said. "I didn't know she didn't drink scotch."

"There, you see?" Stella said. She grabbed the captain's arm.

Marco shifted uneasily. "There was one strange thing about that glass, sir," he said. "We of course dusted for fingerprints.

Not that that'll do much good. Anyone who was at the dinner would have left prints. But the strange thing was there were no fingerprints at all on the visitor's glass of scotch."

Captain Bonar drew in a quick, sharp, gasp of air. His jaw tensed.

"Oh, Gran!" Max jumped up and down excitedly, her ponytail bouncing up and down with her. "We've just got to find out who had that drink with Garvey. Come on." She grabbed Stella's arm and tugged her towards the door. "These two aren't going to help. We'll investigate ourselves."

Great balls of fur! I launched a loud yowling protest. They could get themselves into even more trouble.

"Wait!" Captain Bonar caught them before they could leave. He sighed heavily. This time there was no doubt it was a sigh of exasperation. "Alright, we'll investigate." He paused. "Make that *I'll* investigate. You can sit in on the interviews if you like as long as you promise not to interfere. I'll ask the questions. Understood?"

"Understood," Stella said. She threw her arms around the captain. "Oh, Gideon, I knew you would help."

Paul Marco stared at the captain. "But, sir," he said. His voice crackled with disbelief. "We really ought to leave this to the proper authorities."

Captain Bonar raised himself to his full height and towered above Marco.

"I'm the captain, Marco. I give the orders," he said. "You take over on the bridge. I'll take over the investigation."

"Yes, sir." Marco could barely squeeze the words through his tightly pressed lips. "Highly irregular," he muttered as he turned his back and stiffly marched out of the room.

I, too, clamped my lips together and stared at the captain. It was indeed highly irregular for the captain to insist on handling the investigation himself. Had he done it to impress Stella? Or did he have an even darker motive? Was he perhaps afraid of what someone else might find out when they began asking questions?

The boat tilted, and I slid across the cage, my nose banging against the grid work. The bottles on the captain's bar rattled, stirring up a memory. Only a few days ago I'd seen Captain Bonar pour himself a drink from one of those bottles. He'd leaned back in his chair, propped his feet on the desk, and twirled the glass between his fingers, causing the ice to clink annoyingly against the rim. That glass had contained scotch. Stella's hero, the great captain himself, was a scotch drinker with a very strong motive to get rid of Leroy Garvey.

CHAPTER 17

MAX AND STELLA WERE already huddled around the captain's desk by the time the door closed on the disapproving staff captain.

"Let's make a list of all the scotch drinkers who knew Garvey," Max said. "Have you got something we can write on, Gran?"

Stella dug into her voluminous tote bag and pulled out the offensive notepad depicting a cat riding a polar bear. Totally ridiculous. But so was the idea of Stella and Max trying to unmask the killer. That was not only ridiculous, but dangerous. Didn't they realize poking around, trying to solve a murder, could get a person killed? I yowled my objections.

"Oh, do be quiet, Paws," Stella said. "We're trying to think."

That's the problem. Thinking was not her strong suit at the best of times, and if Jo's fate depended on Stella's thinking, then Jo was in more serious trouble than she knew. I yowled even louder.

Captain Bonar joined in my objections.

"Now, ladies," he said, his voice gently reproving. "Didn't I say I'd do the investigating?"

"Then sit down and help us," Max ordered. She scooted her chair over to make room for him at the desk.

"Oh, yes, Gideon, do help us," Stella added. She patted the

chair beside her in a shameless invitation for the captain to sit next to her.

What was the matter with the woman's taste? How could she possibly want that wily captain sitting that close to her? I yowled another objection, but she ignored me.

"You know the passengers better than we do, Gideon," she said. "Which ones knew Garvey? And which ones drank scotch?"

Captain Bonar sighed and ran his hands through his thick wavy hair.

"Alright," he said, his voice heavy with resignation. "I guess I know when I'm beaten." He sank into the chair, slid it even closer to Stella, and rested his elbows on the desk. "What have you got so far?" he asked.

"Duh," Max said, tapping the empty notepad. As if the scorn in her voice wasn't enough, she rolled her eyes and stared at the captain as though he'd lost a few marbles. I'd have done the same except no one was paying any attention to me.

"We've only just sat down," Max said.

She pulled the pad closer to her and printed SUSPECTS in large letters at the top of the page, her pen pressing hard into the paper.

"You can leave Jo and me off the list," Stella said. "Neither one of us can stand scotch."

The captain rested his head on his tightly clasped hands, but not before I caught a patronizing smirk slip across his face. Captain Bonar was only humoring Stella and Max. This whole investigation was a mere charade.

The boat tilted, and I slid backwards, crashing into the bars of my cage. The offensive notepad slipped out of Max's hands and tumbled across the desk. Stella and Max both shrieked as their chairs slid across the floor. Max slid into the desk. Stella would have slid into my cage if the captain hadn't stretched out an arm and pulled both her and her chair towards him. His other hand darted out and grabbed the notepad as it slid off the edge of the desk.

Licking furiously at my bruised tail, I dared a quick peek out the window. Slashing rain and gigantic waves lapped furiously at the boat. No wonder it was rocking. Captain Bonar ought to be on the bridge, not trying to impress Stella by carrying on this pretence of an investigation. It was obvious he'd already made up his mind to pin the murder on Jo, whether she was guilty or not.

I glared unblinkingly at the captain, but neither my accusing stare nor the rocking boat seemed to have any effect on his composure. His one arm now firmly around Stella, he slid the notepad across the desk to Max.

"Angus Lloyd considers himself a connoisseur of scotch," he said, as though the rocking boat were of no concern to him at all. "Bored me to death with his listing of the various sorts and how they were made."

"Angus Lloyd," Stella repeated. She took a deep breath and tried to appear as calm as the captain. "Write that down, Max," she ordered, tapping the notepad.

Max scribbled down the name.

I tried to tell them to add the captain to the list, but all three of them shushed me.

"Do be quiet, Paws," Stella said.

"And Tyler Onslow," Max exclaimed excitedly. She scribbled his name to the list. "I've seen him drink a whole bottle in one night," she added, her eyes sparkling. "He could barely stand up afterward. I had to call Akito to help me get him back to his room."

"Well, Tyler might like his scotch," the captain said. "But

somehow I can't see him sitting down with Garvey to drink it, can you?"

"Add his name anyway," Stella ordered.

The boat tilted again, and I slid to the other side of the cage. My nose banged against the bars. Stella's chair slid even closer to Captain Bonar's, although I hadn't thought that possible. He took the opportunity to throw his other arm around her as well.

"Lorne Akito enjoys a scotch now and then," he said. "I've shared a bottle with him on occasion."

Shiver me whiskers! Could the clue get any clearer? I yowled for their attention. Captain Bonar had just admitted he was a scotch drinker. Why didn't they add his name? I yowled even louder.

"Paws, be quiet!" Stella ordered.

"Maybe we should cover him with a blanket," Captain Bonar said. That sly smirk slid across his face again, and he winked at me. "That's how they shut up noisy parrots."

He should know. Every notorious pirate owns a noisy parrot. Captain Bonar might dress in white, and Stella might think of him as her charming white knight, but under that gallant white armor beat a heart as devious as that of old Davey Jones himself.

I closed my eyes and pretended to ignore the captain and his two cohorts. Let them make their list. I had a list of my own, and Captain Bonar's name sat right at the top of it. I returned to loosening the hinge on my cage. I might be trapped for now, but somehow I'd get out of this cage, and when I did, I'd find all the evidence I needed to sink Captain Bonar in his own turbulent ocean of deceit.

CHAPTER 18

THEY ADDED A FEW more names to their list.

"Berti Onslow!" Stella exclaimed. She jumped out of her chair, leaned across the table, and tapped the notepad in front of Max. "Berti Onslow did it! Write her name down. Top of the list!"

Max looked doubtful. "I don't know, Gran," she said. "From what I've seen of Berti Onslow, she wanted to marry Leroy Garvey, not kill him."

"But that's it. Don't you see?" Stella said. Stella looked to the captain for support.

Captain Bonar leaned back in his chair, raised an eyebrow, and let another patronizing smile spread across his face.

"Seems to me she'd be more likely to murder Jo than Garvey," he said.

"Not if Garvey threatened to ruin her career if she didn't quit pestering him," Stella argued. "And of course she'd frame Jo for the murder. Killing two birds with one stone. Don't you see? Everything fits."

Max added Berti Onslow's name to the list.

"And I'm adding Patricia Garvey," she said, her ponytail flicking defiantly. "She's the one who stands to gain the most from his death, isn't she?"

Cat-o-Nine-Tails! Their list was getting more absurd by the

minute. Berti Onslow loved money. She wouldn't kill the goose that might lay her golden egg. And Patricia? Surely Patricia couldn't kill her father. And besides, she didn't even drink scotch.

I had to get out of here and find out who the real culprit was. I attacked the hinges of my cage with everything I had— all four feet, everyone of my claws. I even twisted myself into the shape of an upside down pretzel and gnawed at the thing with my teeth. It was slow and exhausting work with very little progress, made even more frustrating by the constant demands of Stella and Max ordering me to settle down.

When Max and Stella added Miriam Turner to the list, despite the captain's loud protest that she couldn't possibly have had anything to do with it, Captain Bonar called an end to the list making. He pulled his cell phone out of his pocket and punched a number.

"Akito," he barked into the phone. "Report to my quarters pronto, and bring Alvin with you."

Lorne Akito had no sooner arrived, than the wind and waves launched a new attack on the ship, rocking it from side to side. Akito slid into the door frame like a drunken sailor.

"Good morning, sir!" he said. He attempted to pull himself upright. "Looks like we're in for a little rock and roll today." He tried one of his hearty laughs, but it fell flat. Even his earring failed to jangle.

He'd exchanged his pirate's costume for a pristine white officer's uniform. If he was hoping that would make him look more angelic to escape the captain's wrath, he should have lost the gold-hooped earring and that wide, toothy smile that hid a multitude of sins.

"Look, Captain," he said, the toothy smile spreading across his cherubic face, and his eyes pleading for understanding.

"I'm truly sorry, sir. I shouldn't have let Alvin play in the band. I tried to stop the two of them from switching roles, but some people are simply unstoppable." He glared at Max, who stuck her tongue out at him from behind the captain's back.

Captain Bonar frowned. "Where is Alvin?" he asked. "I told you to bring him with you."

"I would have, sir, if I could have found him," Akito said. His head bobbled slightly, and his earring jangled nervously. "He didn't show up for his shift. No one has seen him since he stormed out of the rehearsal dinner last night."

The captain's frown deepened. He pulled out his cell phone, punched in a number, waited a few minutes, snapped it shut, and shoved it back in his pocket.

"He's not answering his cell phone either," he said worriedly.

Stella sprang to her feet and tugged on the captain's sleeve. "Never mind all that, Captain," she interrupted. "We're in the midst of an investigation, remember? You needn't worry about Alvin. He's just tucked himself away somewhere to think. That's what teenage boys do when they're upset. I'll help you look for him later. Right now we have questions for this young man." She pointed at Lorne Akito.

Akito took a step backward. "Questions for me?" he asked warily. "About what?"

"About the murder, of course," Max piped up, giving him one of her impudent grins. "We want to know if you killed Leroy Garvey."

Akito's head snapped back, his eyes widened, and his earring jangled in alarm. His colorful exclamation was swallowed up in the sound of rattling bottles on the bar as the ship once more tilted.

Max's chair slid across the room. Her notepad fell to the floor with a clatter that made me jump and hit my head on the roof of my cage. Stella tottered precariously on her stilted heels and would have crashed headlong into my cage if the captain hadn't once more come to her rescue. He ushered her back to her chair at the desk.

"Let me ask the questions," the captain said.

He invited Akito to have a seat, but Akito smiled nervously and clung more tightly to the bar rail.

"I prefer to stand, sir, if you don't mind," Akito said. "Can keep my balance better, if you know what I mean." He gave a nervous laugh. His head bobbled slightly. His earring tinkled briefly, but the sound soon lost itself among the bottles rattling on the bar behind him.

Captain Bonar, too, preferred to remain upright, but instead of standing, he paced back and forth across the room, rolling with the roll of the boat.

I grabbed the bars of my cage and tried to stay in place, but my rear end slid back and forth like a windshield wiper.

"Was Garvey alone when you came back with his bottle of scotch?" the captain asked.

Akito nodded, and his earring jangled in agreement. "Yes, sir," he said. "And he was in a thunderous mood. I left the scotch and scurried out of there as fast as I could." He fiddled with his earring to stifle the jangling.

He was obviously hiding something. I yowled a warning to the interrogators, but only Max seemed to understand. She looked at me. Her eyes brightened with anticipation. Resting her elbows on the table, and her head on her folded hands, she looked up at Akito and gave him another saucy grin.

"He yelled at you, didn't he?" she said.

Akito scowled at her. "Of course he yelled at me," he admitted.

"What about?" Stella asked.

Akito's earring jangled even more frantically as he turned his scowl on Stella.

"I was nervous, okay?" he said. "That man was dangerous to be around when he was in a good mood. But he was in a rage, and I didn't want to be there. I guess my hand shook a bit when I went to pour his drink. I spilled a little of his precious scotch. Set him off like I'd lit a match under him. The man was a lunatic. Told me this whole fiasco was my fault."

"He threatened you, didn't he?" Stella exclaimed. She jumped out of her chair in her excitement. The ship tilted, and she stumbled forward. Once more the captain caught her to prevent her from falling, but Stella was too intent on her line of questioning to stay caught in his embrace. She pulled away from him and tottered drunkenly across the swaying floor toward Akito.

"I knew he'd threatened someone," she said. Her eyes sparkled. "You were sitting there drinking a scotch with him. He took off his glasses, tapped them incessantly on that huge diamond ring of his, leaned into your face." Stella leaned closer to Akito. "And then he uttered his threat," she said.

"Drinking with him?" Lorne exclaimed.

He tried to back away from Stella, but she lost her balance and slid right into him. She threw her arms around his neck and held on for dear life. Akito's earring jangled in double time as he stared down at the top of her head.

"Are you crazy, Ma'am?" he shouted. "Leroy Garvey is the last person I'd sit down to have a drink with. And I'm the last person he'd invite to have one with him. He told me to get out and make sure no one else came in. He wanted to be alone to think, he said. So I got out."

Captain Bonar hurried over and dragged Stella off of Akito.

"I thought we agreed that I'd do the questioning," the

captain said. He steered Stella back to her chair, settled her into it a little more forcefully than he'd done earlier, and then turned back to Akito.

"Did Garvey have Mrs. Bellamy's scarf when you were there?" the captain asked.

"Mrs. Bellamy's scarf?" Akito asked. His face screwed up into a thoughtful frown as he tried to remember. "No," he said. "Garvey didn't have it. It was caught on the railing just outside the door, flapping like mad." A faint smile flitted across Akito's face and then disappeared just as quickly. "I thought about rescuing it," he admitted. "But I had my hands full."

"And Garvey was alive when you left him?" the captain asked.

"Oh, yes, sir," Akito said.

"Really, Captain," Max interrupted. "What kind of question is that? Do you really think he's going to admit the man was dead when he left?"

Captain Bonar scowled at Max, and then turned back to Lorne Akito.

"Anyone see you leave?" he asked.

"I nearly ran into Angus Lloyd on my way out the door. He could tell you Garvey was alive and in full voice when I left."

"Angus Lloyd!" Stella exclaimed. She snatched the notepad out of Max's hand and marked a huge star beside Angus Lloyd's name. "Then it must have been Angus Lloyd who killed him."

"But you might want to talk to Tyler Onslow, too, sir," Akito said.

"Tyler Onslow?" Stella questioned. She drew a large question mark beside Tyler's name on the list.

I yowled my objection. My friend Tyler was no killer.

"Any particular reason for your suggestion?" Captain Bonar asked.

"Well, sir." Akito shifted from one foot to the other, stared at the floor, and fidgeted with his earring. "I uh," he stammered, and then shuffled his feet some more.

Shiver me whiskers, what was wrong with the man? I'd never seen Lorne Akito fumble for words before. I stopped gnawing on the hinge to my cage, and peered through the bars. What was he about to admit to?

"You what?" the captain asked, his patience wearing thin. "Spit it out, man."

Akito drew in a deep breath, raised his head, stared the captain in the eye, and blurted it out.

"I know I shouldn't have done it, sir. It was unconscionable. But I was just so angry with Garvey. What right did he have yelling at everyone? Accusing them? Threatening them? Ordering them about like he was king of the underworld? He'd said he didn't want to see anyone, but when I was walking past the Club Lounge, I just happened to see Tyler and Patricia having a drink. And who would Garvey hate to see more than anyone else on the ship?"

"Tyler Onslow," Stella interjected.

Akito nodded. His earring jangled. "So I told Tyler that Garvey wanted to see him."

"And did Tyler go see Garvey?" Max asked.

"I don't know," Akito said. "He wasn't going to at first, but Patricia got so excited. She was convinced her father had changed his mind about Tyler and wanted to apologize."

"Of course Tyler went to see Garvey," Stella said. "He's infatuated with Patricia. He'd do anything she asked him to." She sprang up from her chair and grabbed hold of the captain's sleeve. "Call him in, Captain. Talk to him."

"All in good time," the captain said. His voice was thin

with impatience. "I'm the one handling this investigation, remember?"

He set her back into her chair, this time far from gently, and turned back to Akito.

"That's it for now then, Akito. You can go," he said.

He dropped into the chair beside Stella and rubbed his face with his hands as though trying to wipe away all the worry lines.

Max smirked up at Lorne Akito, her eyes dancing, her red ponytail bouncing. "But don't leave the boat without our permission," she ordered in a sing-song voice.

Akito scowled at her, and then turned back to the captain.

"If you ask me, sir, you might want to interrogate that little minx," he said, pointing at Max. "She and that son of yours probably know a whole lot more about this than they're letting on."

The captain's jaw tensed. "What do you mean by that?" he demanded.

"Well, sir, you have to admit, Alvin was pretty angry with Garvey," Akito said. "It seems he blamed Garvey for his mother abandoning him." Akito shrugged. His earring jangled. "Who knows maybe things got a little heated and Alvin lost control."

The captain's face was now alarmingly red. He leapt to his feet with a bellow of rage.

Akito took a step backward. His head bobbled. His earring jangled frantically.

"How dare you?" the captain shouted. "My son is no killer."

He grabbed Akito's arm and shoved him roughly toward the door.

"Out!" he ordered.

Cat-o-nine-tails! Captain Bonar had quite a temper when roused. I peered at him through the bars of my cage as he shoved Akito out of the room and slammed the door shut. And he had every bit as strong a motive as Alvin to kill Leroy Garvey, perhaps stronger. Maybe now Max and Stella would add him to their list.

I yowled my suggestion, but they didn't even hear me. They were gaping at the captain in wide-eyed disbelief.

CHAPTER 19

A SHARP RAP ON the door broke the stunned silence. Angus Lloyd burst into the room almost before the captain had time to open the door.

I couldn't stop the growl that formed in the pit of my stomach. Angus Lloyd, with his greased-back hair and well-trimmed moustache, his expensive suit and his gold watch, might look the part of the successful businessman, but he was nothing more than a cat-killing thug. Hadn't he tossed me overboard without the least twinge of conscience? If he could kill a cat, he could easily turn on his own master. If I hadn't already made up my mind the captain had done it, I would put Angus Lloyd at the top of my list.

"What's all this nonsense about an investigation, Captain?" Angus demanded, his voice clipped and arrogant. His black eyebrows creased together in a thunderous frown. "It's clear that Jo Bellamy killed Leroy. I have more important things to do than take part in this ridiculous investigation."

The ship rolled, and Angus grabbed for the stair railing to keep from sliding off his feet.

"And it seems to me so do you," he added. He looked pointedly up the stairs that led to the bridge above.

Before he could say anything more, he doubled over in

a round of sneezing. Rubbing his streaming eyes, he looked suspiciously around the room until he caught sight of me.

"The cat!" he shrieked. His voice rose to heights even Stella's couldn't reach. "Get rid of that cat!" Angus shrieked again. He pointed a finger at me as though I were the devil, or perhaps a ghost cat risen from the depths of the sea.

I hissed right back at him. Angus Lloyd's black eyebrows raced for the fringe of his greased-back hair. I lunged toward him, but my nose smacked into the edge of my cage. Hissing and snarling, I reached through the bars, my claws screaming for action.

Angus Lloyd backed as far into the stair railing as he could.

"Inspector Paws!" Stella shouted, her voice laden with shock.

I barely heard her. I lunged at the bars again. My wheeled cage jerked towards Angus Lloyd. Stella jumped between us.

"Stop that this minute," she ordered.

She shoved the cage back to its place by the window and planted herself right in front of me. How dare she take Angus Lloyd's side over mine? Couldn't she see that man wasn't to be trusted?

Angus Lloyd doubled over in another fit of sneezing, and I renewed my efforts to loosen the hinge on my cage. If only I could get out of here, I'd give that cat-killing coward a swipe or two of these claws he wouldn't soon forget. He'd be running out of here so fast the grease from his slicked-back hair would splat Stella in the face.

Even with me locked in a cage, Angus tried to make a run for it, but the captain barred his way.

"Just a couple of questions before you leave, Angus," the captain said. "Lorne Akito says you went to see Leroy Garvey after everyone left. Akito says he ran into you on his way out."

"He did," Angus said. His voice was muffled by the sleeve

of his jacket as he tried to stifle another sneeze. I was pleased to see his eyes streaming with tears. "He ran right into me. Nearly knocked me off my feet, he was so anxious to get out of that room. Garvey was in one of his rages, bellowing in full voice. I was almost afraid to go in."

"Why did you go in?" Captain Bonar asked.

"I don't believe that's any of your business, Captain."

Captain Bonar pulled himself up to his full height.

"Everything is my business when there's a murder investigation," he barked.

"It's certainly not their business." Angus pointed to Max and Stella.

Max, still sitting at the desk with her ridiculous notepad, rested her chin in her hands and gave Angus an impudent smile. "Do you have something to hide, Mr. Lloyd?" she asked.

"No, I have nothing to hide," Angus shouted. He burst into another round of sneezes. "Garvey phoned me," he mumbled when the sneezing fit subsided, his head once more buried in his sleeve. "Garvey asked me to bring him his laptop," he added.

"His laptop?" Captain Bonar sounded puzzled.

"You do know what a laptop is, don't you, Captain?" Angus asked. Even his sleeve couldn't bury the sarcasm.

"There was no laptop at the crime scene," Captain Bonar said.

"No laptop?" Angus jerked his head out of hiding. "Now that does concern me," he said. "Wouldn't want that laptop getting in the wrong hands. I took it to him. He had it when I left. We need to track it down, Captain."

Stella's bleached blond curls bobbed in front of me as she shoved away from my cage.

"He's trying to sidetrack you, Captain," Stella said. "He

killed Garvey and now he wants to send you on a wild goose chase after some laptop."

I buried my head in my paws and tried not to peek out at Stella. Didn't she know she was making a fool of herself? First, she'd been certain it was Berti Onslow. And then, it was poor Akito. And now she'd fixed the murder on Angus Lloyd. Next she'd be claiming it was a conspiracy, and they'd all done it together.

She darted across to Angus Lloyd. "You sat down and had a drink with him, didn't you Mr. Lloyd?" she said.

"No, I did not."

"Did he threaten you?" Stella barely waited for his answer. "Did you kill him?"

Angus tried to back away from her, but the stair railing held him in place.

"This is most irregular, Captain," he said. "Are you letting civilians do your questioning? Garvey was alive and well when I left him."

"We only have your word for that," Max piped up. Her red ponytail flicked insolently.

"You'll just have to take my word for it then, won't you?" Angus said. "Now if you'll excuse me, Captain, I have more important things to attend to. A business like Garvey's doesn't hold together by itself, especially when the CEO dies from unnatural causes."

He slammed the door as he went out, and then popped it back open.

"Find that laptop, Captain," he ordered. "And I suggest you look close to home. I saw that thieving son of yours lurking on deck when I left Garvey last night."

The captain's face reddened.

"My son did not kill anyone," he shouted "And he's not a thief!"

"He tried to steal my briefcase, didn't he?" Angus Lloyd said.

He quickly disappeared before the captain could respond. Captain Bonar turned to Max.

"It wasn't Alvin who tried to steal that briefcase," he said. "It was you, wasn't it?"

He grabbed Max's shoulders.

"You know where Alvin is, don't you?" he said. "Tell me," he ordered. "Tell me right now."

Max's usual defiance deserted her as she looked up at the captain's angry face. Her eyes grew large and frightened.

"I don't know where he is, Captain," she said. "Honest. I haven't seen him since he left the rehearsal dinner last night."

Stella leapt to Max's defence.

"Stop it, Gideon! Stop it, right now!" she shouted. She grabbed his arm and dragged him away from Max. "Max doesn't know where he is. There's no need to brow beat her."

"I'm sorry," Captain Bonar mumbled. He let go of Max, paced to the window and leaned his head against the cold window pane.

Stella joined him. Her voice dropped to a more gentle tone.

"Don't worry, Gideon," she said. "Alvin will turn up in his own good time."

Captain Bonar sighed, pulled his cell phone out of his pocket, punched in a number, and waited for a few minutes. "Call me back, Alvin," he pleaded. He snapped the phone shut and shoved it back into his pocket.

Max slid out of her chair and joined the others by the window. Her usual bounce was missing. She placed a hand hesitantly on the captain's arm.

"He didn't do it, you know," she said as though trying to convince herself. "Alvin couldn't kill anyone. I know he couldn't."

CHAPTER 20

TYLER ONSLOW WAS NEXT on their list of suspects. He slouched in the doorway, looking not only ill at ease but unshaven, bleary-eyed, and disheveled, as though he'd had a long night and hadn't yet made it to bed. The jacket of his white tuxedo was rumpled, and his mass of golden curls stuck out in every which direction as though he'd put his hand in an electric socket.

His eyes brightened at the sight of me. He limped across the room and rested an arm on the top of my cage. By the looks of him, he needed something to support him, even my wobbly cage, if only to keep him from toppling over.

"Hi, there, Tiger," he slurred. "How are they treating you?"

Better than they'd been treating him by the looks of it. He smelled strongly of scotch. His left eye was black and swollen. A purple bruise covered the cheek below it. I yowled in sympathy.

"Afraid we're the ones with the questions, Tyler, not the cat," Captain Bonar said, with more than a trace of impatience.

The trio of interrogators lined up against the window staring at him accusingly seemed to snap Tyler out of his inebriation. He straightened up and stared back at them as though they were about to make him walk the plank.

His hand continued to play nervously with the hinge of my cage. He twisted the metal piece that held the hinge together.

138

It was definitely loosening. I purred my gratitude. He dipped a hand in the cage and ruffled my fur. A button was missing from his cuff. That's where I'd seen that gold button. Great balls of fur! Surely Tyler wasn't the killer.

He pulled his hand out of my cage and returned to unwinding the piece of metal.

"Yes, I did go to see Garvey," he said. "Big mistake." He rubbed his blackened eye. "Akito told me Garvey wanted to see me. I wouldn't have gone if Patricia hadn't begged me to. She thought maybe he'd changed his mind. I was pretty sure he hadn't, but when a girl asks you do something, you don't want to appear too cowardly, do you?" He tried a lop-sided grin, but it slipped away almost before it had appeared.

"And did you sit down and have a scotch with him?" Captain Bonar asked.

"Sit down with him?" Tyler's voice rose in amazement. "I didn't get a chance." His fingers moved even faster on the hinge.

"Did he threaten you?" Stella asked. "Twirl his eye glasses?"

He stopped playing with the hinge of my cage, took a step towards Stella, and pointed at his swollen eye.

"No," he said. "He belted me one."

"So you picked up the ice sculpture and threw it at him," Max said, her ponytail bouncing with excitement.

Tyler's eyes widened. "Are you kidding? I couldn't get anywhere near any ice sculpture. I just ran for my life. The man was a maniac. I barely escaped. Had to crawl out the window."

"I suppose this would be yours, then?" the captain asked. He showed him the button.

Tyler looked at the button, and then looked down at his cuff.

"Yeah," he muttered. "Must have come off when I went through the window." He staggered over to the trio of interrogators. His voice rose pleadingly. "I didn't kill him. You've got to believe me," he said.

"Did you see anyone?" Stella asked. "Hear anything?"

Tyler took a step away from them.

"I'd rather not say," he muttered. He licked his lips, ran a hand across his face, and looked nervously at the captain.

"You've got to tell us, Tyler," Stella pleaded. She placed a hand on his arm. Tyler jumped back at her touch.

"It's just that you now appear to be the last one who saw him alive," Stella said.

Tyler again looked anxiously toward the captain. "I didn't kill him," he said. "But I saw ..."

The door banged open, and Berti Onslow burst into the room. Her quivering golden curls, flushed face, and angry eyes gave her the appearance of an avenging angel.

"Don't you say another word, Tyler Onslow," she ordered. Her usually melodic voice breathed fire.

Tyler spun around at the sound of it, and then grabbed for my cage to keep from sprawling on the floor. My cage banged into the window, and I looked nervously at the angry waves. But they were nothing compared to the torrent of anger issuing from Berti Onslow's tiny frame as she marched across the room, grabbed Tyler by the arm, and hauled him toward the door.

She looked over her shoulder, her eyes piercing the trio of interrogators.

"And you lot ought to be ashamed of yourselves," she said. "Harassing innocent passengers. You can see for yourselves my son is in no condition to be interrogated. Believe me, Captain Bonar, the cruise line is going to hear about this."

She dragged the stumbling Tyler into the hallway and slammed the door behind them.

The three interrogators stared silently at the closed door.

Captain Bonar was the first to turn away. He paced over to my cage, slid it back to its allotted place, and then planted himself firmly in front of me, grabbing both sides of the cage as if for support.

"Perhaps she's right," he said, not daring to look at either Stella or Max. "This is getting much too complicated. We need to leave this investigation to the proper authorities."

"But we can't stop now!" Stella protested.

She snatched the notepad from out of Max's grasp and hurried over to the captain.

"We've still got all these people to question," she said. She jabbed a finger at the names on the list, and then started reading them off. "*Berti Onslow.*"

Captain Bonar shook his head in disbelief.

"Surely even you can't expect me to question her after that," he said.

Max jumped up and down excitedly, her ponytail bouncing with her.

"Not Berti," she said. "We need to talk to Tyler again. He knows something. He saw the killer. He was just about to tell us."

Max grabbed Stella's arm. "Come on, Gran," she said. "We don't need the captain. We can do this ourselves."

Stella looked hesitantly at the captain, then breathed in deeply, and tossed her head in defiance.

"She's absolutely right, Captain Bonar," she said. We don't need your help."

She braced her shoulders and marched after Max, her spiky heels clicking with the rapid staccato of a deadly machine gun.

"Wait!" Captain Bonar called. He raced for the door and tried to stop them.

I could have told him he was wasting his energy. When

Stella and Max made up their minds to do something, there was no stopping them.

The door slammed in his face.

The captain raised his hands to his head and pulled at his hair. He paced the room in circles, muttering under his breath, and finally came to a stop by the side of my cage. He stared in at me.

"So what do you think I should do, Inspector Paws?" he asked.

I stared into his eyes. Perhaps if I stared long enough and hard enough, I'd be able to read his devious mind. Had he killed Leroy Garvey? Tyler had certainly looked at the captain rather nervously when he was about to tell who he had seen with Garvey. Was that because it was the captain himself he'd seen?

Confess your crimes, that's what you should do. I yowled at him loudly.

The captain gave a scornful laugh, shook his head as though in disbelief, and sauntered over to the window. Spray from the rain and giant waves splashed the window in front of his face, temporarily obscuring the view. He leaned his head against the glass.

"I've been too long at sea," he muttered. "Now I'm talking to cats."

Too bad he wouldn't listen to them. I yowled at him again.

"They'll have me locked up."

As they should. I yowled in agreement. And I would give them every bit of help I could.

I sank to the bottom of my cage, rested my head on my paws, and pondered my next move.

CHAPTER 21

THE FIRST STEP WAS to get out of this cage. Tyler had already loosened the top hinge of the door. I worked diligently on the bottom hinge, while the captain paced back and forth across the room. His sea-faring legs barely wobbled when the ship tilted, but I was continually sliding to the rear of the cage and dragging myself back to work on the hinge. It was exhausting work and seemed to be taking much too long. Even when I got out of this cage, I'd still need to find a way out of the captain's cabin. And then I'd have to find Tyler.

Max was right. Tyler knew who the killer was. He would have told us if Berti hadn't interrupted. And that was the question I was pondering as I gnawed at the stubborn hinge. Why had Berti stopped Tyler from talking? Had she killed Garvey? That hardly seemed likely. She'd wanted to marry Garvey — or at least Garvey's money. She was all about money, and there'd be no money coming her way with Garvey dead. Unless ...

I could barely contain my excitement as the thought entered my mind. My paw slipped. The sharp point of the loosened hinge dug into the pad of my foot. I gave a small mewl, and then licked away the blood.

That was it! Berti Onslow wanted to use Tyler's knowledge to blackmail the killer. Cat-o-Nine-Tails! Didn't she know someone who's killed once won't hesitate to kill again? Tyler was in danger.

With even more urgency, I returned to the task of loosening the hinge. I mewled in relief as it popped out of its casing and pinged onto the floor.

Across the room Captain Bonar yanked his cell phone out of his pocket and stabbed at a button. I could hear the buzz of the phone as it rang on the other end, and then Alvin's recorded voice saying, "Not here. Leave a message." Even his answering machine sounded sullen.

"Call me, Alvin, please," the captain pleaded. "You don't have to tell me where you're hiding. I just need to know you're safe."

He stuffed the phone back into his pocket, paced three times around the room, and then stopped in front of my cage. I froze in place. Was all my work for nothing? Would he notice the dismantled hinge?

But his mind was too preoccupied. He rubbed his temples and ran his hands through his wavy hair.

"This is no good, Inspector Paws," he said. "I'm going out to look for him."

He grabbed his jacket and headed for the door.

I sprang to my feet and shoved against the bars. I needed to beat him to the door if I was going to escape. I'd barely squeezed my head and one leg out of the cage, when Miriam Turner burst into the room, nearly knocking the captain off his feet. I quickly pulled my head back into the cage. The bars might not be all that strong, but I needed at least some protection between me and that siren of doom.

"Gideon Bonar, have you lost your mind?" she stormed. "Interviewing people? That's not your job. That's up to the authorities."

Captain Bonar took a step back from her, and then changed his mind. He pulled himself to his full height and looked down his nose at her.

"I am the authority on this ship, Miriam, or had you forgotten?" he said.

"It's not your job to solve crimes," Miriam said. "Anyway, it's obvious Jo Bellamy killed the man. And who could blame her?"

Obvious? I hissed menacingly. Miriam jumped.

"Gracious, Gideon! Haven't you gotten rid of that cat yet?" she said.

"What would you have me do, Miriam?" the captain asked. "Throw him overboard? Where's your compassion?"

Compassion? This woman had less compassion than a hungry polar bear. I doubt if there was anyone on the boat she couldn't find fault with, expect perhaps Patricia. And that was puzzling. She seemed to have a soft spot for that girl. Did she really like Patricia? Or was she using Patricia to get back at Garvey?

"And what possible business is it of yours if I choose to investigate this matter?" the captain asked.

"You could get yourself into trouble," Miriam said. "I heard Officer Marco muttering as much. He said it was highly irregular. Said you were jeopardizing your career."

"He did, did he?" The captain's face looked as threatening as those angry waves lapping relentlessly at the ship.

The ship lifted and rolled. Miriam caught hold of my cage for support. I hissed and slunk as far away from her as I could.

"I'll have a word with Officer Marco," the captain continued. "Both you and he need to remember that I'm the captain, and I'll question who I wish. Now, if you'll excuse me."

He put a hand on Miriam's shoulder and pointed to the door.

"Oh, Gideon," Miriam's voice softened. "I just don't want you to ruin your career. You've got Alvin to think about. And besides, it's just so obvious that Jo Bellamy killed him."

"Not obvious," the captain said. "There were others who could have done it."

"Like who?"

"Tyler Onslow, for one," the captain said. "He was sporting quite a black eye. He said Garvey had belted him one."

Miriam scoffed. "Really, Gideon, you're clutching at straws. You can't tell me Tyler Onslow would exert himself enough to kill anyone."

Captain Bonar shrugged.

"Well he did say he barely escaped with his life. He said he had to crawl out of the window. We found this, which seems to verify that part of his story at least."

The captain picked up the packet containing the button and held it out to Miriam. Miriam stared at it. A frown puckered her brow.

"Anyway, it doesn't explain Jo's scarf," Miriam said. "Jo must have been there. Why else would Garvey have her scarf in his hand?"

"Someone else could have brought it in," the captain said. "Anyone could have retrieved it from the railing."

"Oh, come on, Gideon. You don't really think someone deliberately killed Garvey, and then framed Jo by leaving her scarf in Garvey's hand?"

"Of course not," the captain agreed. "This murder wasn't premeditated. No one could have relied on an ice sculpture as a murder weapon. Much too uncertain. If that piece hadn't broken off and stabbed him in the eye, he might just have suffered a mild concussion."

The captain pulled out a chair, sat down at the bar, and propped his head in his hands.

"I suspect," he continued, "that the murderer sat down with Garvey, likely at Garvey's invitation, and started sipping a glass of expensive scotch. During the course of the conversation, Garvey pulled his glasses out of his pocket, twirled them around in this hand, and issued one of his quiet and chilling threats."

The shiver running up my spine and tingling through each of my whiskers told me the captain was describing exactly what happened. It was as though he himself had been there.

"The murderer lost his temper," the captain continued. "He picked up the ice sculpture and threw it at Garvey."

Captain Bonar slapped his hands on the table, and both Miriam and I jumped.

"We just need to find out who had that scotch with him," Captain Bonar said. He looked sharply at Miriam. "Wasn't you, was it?" he asked.

"Oh, Gideon. Can you really imagine me going anywhere near that man, let alone having a drink with him?"

Captain Bonar sighed, a tired grin flitting across his face

"No, Miriam, I can't," he said. "If you'd killed Garvey it would have been thoroughly planned and a very slow and painful death."

Miriam snorted. "Hmph! This is utter nonsense. Jo Bellamy did it — probably in self defense. And you know it. You're just going through this charade to get on the good side of that widow friend of hers."

The captain smiled. "Stella Clayton, you mean," he said. "Of course I'm doing this for Stella. There's no harm in asking a few questions, is there?"

"Other than to get you fired," Miriam snapped.

The captain shrugged. "Some things are worth the risk, don't you think?"

Miriam shook her head. "There's no fool like an old fool," she said, as she stood up and headed for the door.

She was leaving. I breathed a sigh of relief and inched back closer to the door of my cage. But Miriam stopped with her hand on the door handle and turned back to the captain.

"Look," she said. "Why don't you let me talk to Jo Bellamy. I've had success influencing young women to make the right decisions. Perhaps it'll work on old women, too. I can persuade her to admit she did it in self defense. Save all this bother. A good lawyer could get her off."

"Well..." The captain frowned.

I yowled my disapproval. Surely he wasn't going to let this spirit of doom loose on poor Jo. There was no telling what Jo would do. She was in a frenzied enough state as it was.

"She's raising an unholy hullabaloo down the hall," Miriam said. "Why don't you let me take her on my early morning jog?"

"Oh, I don't think that's such a great idea," the captain protested. "Supposing Jo isn't the killer. Both she and you could be in grave danger. The real killer would be waiting for an opportunity just like this. All he'd have to do is get rid of Jo, make it look like she committed suicide, and he'd be off scot free."

Great balls of fur! I hadn't thought of that. And supposing Captain Bonar was the killer, was that what he intended to do?

"Send a bodyguard along with us," Miriam said. "You really can't keep her cooped up in that room all day."

"A bodyguard?" The captain pondered the thought. His face cleared. He jumped off the bar stool. "Better than that," he said. "I'll come with you. I can look for Alvin at the same time."

He put a hand on Miriam's shoulder and steered her toward the door.

I squeezed through the tight opening of my cage, ignoring the pain of the bars as they scraped down my side, and raced after the captain and his sister. My tail barely cleared the doorway before the door slammed shut.

CHAPTER 22

I COULD HEAR JO as soon as I left the captain's cabin. Her piercing karate yells echoed up and down the corridor, louder than I'd ever heard them, loud enough, in fact, to raise Davey Jones himself from the deep. A wall-shuddering crashing sound followed each shriek as though she were trying to batter down the door to her cabin.

Captain Bonar stopped in mid-stride. His eyes widened with each shuddering blow.

"What on earth is she doing in there?" he asked.

Miriam gave him a superior, know-it-all toss of the head.

"I told you she was raising a royal hullabaloo, didn't I?" she said.

An even louder yell, followed by a blow that shook the very floor of the corridor, goaded the captain into action. He raced for Jo's cabin with Miriam close on his heels. I padded stealthily behind them.

"Calm down, Mrs. Bellamy! Calm down!" the captain shouted, but his shout was drowned out by another of Jo's blood-curdling shrieks.

"Let me out! Let me out!" Jo yelled. She gave the door a bash that threatened to cave it in.

"Step back from the door!" the captain ordered.

Jo's response was another ear-splitting shriek and a thwack

on the door that bent the top hinge. A few more whacks like that and she be out of there. I silently cheered her on.

"Let me talk to her," Miriam said. She shoved the captain away from the door and stepped a little closer. Keeping her voice calm and reasonable, she began to cast her spell.

"You need to get hold of yourself, Mrs. Bellamy," she said. "You're not doing yourself any favors with this sort of action."

There was complete silence from Jo's side of the door. A shiver of foreboding tickled my whiskers. Silence from Jo was not necessarily a good thing.

"We want to let you out for a bit," Miriam continued in her calm, mesmerizing voice. "But you need to promise to calm yourself before we can open the door. Will you do that?"

Still silence from Jo's side.

After a few seconds of silence, the captain took over again.

"Okay, Mrs. Bellamy, I'm going to open the door now," he said. He fumbled in his pocket for his master card key. "Miriam's going for her morning jog. She thought you might want to join her. Get some air you know."

There was still no sound from inside the room.

The captain pushed the card into the slot and warily eased the door open just a crack. Jo let out a karate yell so loud it froze even the blood in my veins. The door crashed fully open slamming the captain against the wall. He slumped to the floor.

Jo burst out of the room like a lace-clad rocket, still wearing the white crocheted dress she'd worn to the rehearsal dinner. She no longer looked like a princess, but some wild creature from a horror movie. The skirt of the dress hung in tatters around her legs where she'd torn it wide open, all the better to do her karate kicks, and the white crochet was no longer white, but streaked with runny mascara, as was Jo's face. Her hair stood in every which direction. For once, Jo wasn't dressed for the role. Or perhaps she was. This certainly looked like the costume for a crazy woman, and Jo was certainly acting even crazier than usual. She raced wildly down the hallway, swinging a broken chair leg, and shrieking as she went.

I raced after her, but halfway down the hallway, I skidded to a stop. Jo was quite capable of looking after herself. Hadn't she just flattened the captain? It was more important for me to keep an eye on the captain himself. Once he picked himself up off the floor, he'd most likely try to silence Tyler.

I retraced my steps. The captain still lay sprawled on the floor, but his sister had disappeared. More proof of her cold siren's heart. You'd think a sister would at least stick around to lick the captain's wounds. After all, it had been her idea to let Jo out, hadn't it?

It looked like it was up to me to get the captain back on his feet. I reluctantly set to work licking his face. It was not a pleasant task. His nose had stopped bleeding, but the blood was crusted all over his face. It wasn't that I was all that keen on reviving him, but the longer we stayed in one spot, the greater the chances of someone spotting me and dumping me back in the brig.

The captain's eyes flickered open. He brushed me off his face as though brushing away a pesky fly.

"You," he said, his voice heavy with disgust. "Gory little thing, aren't you?"

Great hairy fur balls! Did he really think I had enjoyed the job of licking his wounds?

He tried to grab me, but the movement must have brought a renewed attack of pain. He groaned and raised a hand to his head. I dodged out of reach of his arm and wiped his blood off my whiskers, watching him warily from the corner of my eye as he slowly pulled himself upright.

"I suppose she's gone?" he asked.

I wasn't sure if he was talking about Miriam or Jo, but from the way he looked warily around him, I guessed he meant Jo. Surely he didn't think she'd be crazy enough to hang around.

He pulled a handkerchief out of his pocket and dabbed ineffectually at the dried blood that still remained on his face, and then scraped at the blood stain on the sleeve of his jacket.

"I should go back and change," he muttered. "But there's no time. I have to find him."

My ears perked up. It's possible he meant Alvin, but it was equally possible he meant Tyler.

He stuffed the handkerchief into his pocket and headed off. I padded after him, keeping enough distance between us that he couldn't just reach down and scoop me up. He was still muttering to himself. Maybe his head cracking against the wall had damaged his brain.

"Where is he? Where? Where?" he muttered. "Better start at the top and work my way down."

He headed for the elevator. I raced after him and just managed to squeeze in before the door closed. If it was Tyler he was looking for, surely he'd try Tyler's cabin first.

The elevator stopped at Deck 10. Lorne Akito, surrounded by a group of passengers, squeezed into the elevator. They gasped at the sight of the captain.

"Are you okay, Captain Bonar?" Akito asked.

But the captain had spotted something outside the elevator. He shoved Akito roughly aside and elbowed his way off the elevator. I dodged through the trampling feet of the passengers and followed him.

"Alvin!" the captain shouted.

Alvin's sneakers disappeared around the corner. Captain Bonar chased after them. I skidded around the corner after him, but Alvin seemed to have disappeared. This hallway led to Stella's cabin. Had he taken refuge in there with Max? Captain Bonar seemed to have the same thought. He raced down the corridor and around the corner, and then slid to a screeching stop in front of Garvey's old cabin.

Max and Stella were already there. They stood in the open doorway, their mouths gaping, their eyes bulging. I shoved past their ankles and peered into the room to see what they were staring at. Tyler lay sprawled on the floor of the cabin, his feet propping the door open like a macabre door stop. His head was bloodied where someone had bashed his skull with some sort of weapon. Could it have been Jo's chair leg? Berti lay sprawled beyond him in another pool of blood.

A movement at the end of the hallway caught my attention. An apparition clad in tattered lace slid around the corner and drifted slowly toward us. It took a minute before I recognized Jo. Her fit of anxiety seemed to have disappeared now, leaving her drained and calm.

"What are you all looking at?" she asked.

All eyes turned to her in horror.

CHAPTER 23

COULD JO POSSIBLY HAVE killed Tyler and Berti?

I didn't want to believe it, but she'd run out of her jail room like a wild woman on a rampage, wielding that threatening chair leg. And if she'd killed Leroy, and Tyler had seen her, and they were blackmailing her, she'd certainly have both motive and opportunity. And then there's the key. Who else had a key to her old cabin?

A feeling of dread settled in the pit of my stomach. I slid under the steward's trolley parked nearby and watched from the shadows.

"What?" Jo asked. She looked questioningly at the shocked stares of Stella, Max, and the captain, and then looked down at her tattered and soiled gown.

I too looked at her tattered gown. If Jo had killed Tyler and Berti, wouldn't there be blood stains all over that dress? All I could see was dirt and traces of mascara.

"Well, you'd look like this too if you'd been locked in a closet for twenty-four hours," Jo declared defensively. "And if you all would stop gawking and step away from my door, perhaps I could get in to have a shower."

She took a step toward the door, but the captain barred her way.

"I think you've done enough damage in there already," he said.

"What do you mean?" Jo asked. She peered around him. Her eyes widened in shock at the sight of Tyler's battered body sprawled in the doorway.

"You don't think I did that, do you?" she asked. Her voice quivered with shock.

No one replied.

"Stella?" Jo looked questioningly at Stella, and then placed a hand on each of her shoulders. "You don't really believe I'd kill anyone, Stella, do you?"

Stella rubbed her eyes and then shook her head vigorously as if that would shake away all doubt. "Of course not, Jo," she said. "Of course you wouldn't kill anyone." She threw her arms around Jo.

Captain Bonar cleared his throat to get their attention.

"She nearly killed me, didn't she?" he growled.

Jo looked at him apologetically. "Oh, Captain," she said. "I'm so sorry. I'm glad you're okay. You have to understand I wasn't myself. Claustrophobia does strange things to me."

"And the last time I saw you," the captain continued without acknowledging her apology. "You were swinging a chair leg, waving it over your head like a deadly sword. A chair leg could easily have done that," he said.

He used his thumb to point over his shoulder at Tyler's shattered skull.

"But I dropped that chair leg right after I left that room," Jo cried. "Anyone could have picked it up."

She had dropped the chair leg. I clearly remembered ducking it as I chased down the hallway after her. Jo was telling the truth. She hadn't killed Tyler and Berti. But if it wasn't her, who was it? It definitely hadn't been the captain. I'd been right behind him ever since he'd hauled himself up off the floor outside Jo's jail room. I licked my side in disgust and spat out a few dirty hairs. There went my favorite suspect. But if the captain didn't do it, and Jo didn't do it, then who did? An uneasy feeling fluttered into the pit of my stomach as I remembered Alvin disappearing down the hallway. Was this his cart I was hiding under? I had just started to slide out from my hiding place when Miriam Turner's voice sent me scurrying back under the cart.

"Picked up what?" Miriam asked. She'd obviously caught the tail end of Jo's comment. She flicked her hands through her hair, still wet from a shower. Drops of water landed on my nose, and I stifled a sneeze.

"Miriam!" the captain exclaimed. "Where've you been?"

"Jogging, of course," Miriam replied. "You know I always go jogging from 9:00 to 9:30."

"You just left me lying there on the floor and went off jogging?" the captain chided.

"I checked to see you were breathing. You were moaning, so I knew you'd be okay," Miriam said. "And then I went jogging. I like to keep to my schedule, you know."

"I suppose it didn't occur to you to raise the alarm that Jo had escaped and was racing around with a chair leg for a club," the captain said.

"But I thought you'd do that," Miriam replied. "Anyway, I'm here now, aren't I?"

She caught sight of Tyler's body. Her hand went to her mouth. "Oh, my!" she said. "Did she do that? Oh, Gideon, I'm so sorry. I should never have persuaded you to let her out."

"I didn't do it, I tell you," Jo pleaded. A hint of hysteria crept back into her voice.

"Then where have you been, Aunt Jo?" Max asked. These

were her first words since we'd spotted the bodies. Her face was ashen.

"Oh, Max," Jo cried. She turned toward Max, her eyes pleading. "You can't really think I'd do this."

"Whether we believe you could do this or not is of no relevance," the captain said. "We need to know where you've been since you escaped."

Jo looked defiantly at the captain.

"I didn't escape," she said. "You unlocked the door yourself."

The captain's jaw tightened. Jo quickly continued before he could say anything else.

"I came straight up here to find Stella," she said. "I wanted to know what she'd found out about Leroy's killer, but she wasn't here, so I decided to go to Neptune's Loft. See if there were any clues left. Of course there weren't."

"But that room's been blocked off," the captain said. "No one's allowed in there."

"You don't think a locked door would stop me, do you?" Jo said. "I crawled in the window." Her face clouded over. "Wish I hadn't though," she added. "The room held nothing but sad memories. Today would have been our wedding day if things had gone differently." She sighed, and then shrugged. "It is what it is, though, isn't it? So I came back down here to see if Stella was back yet. And what do I find? You lot huddled around my door accusing me of more murders."

She was right. They were going to accuse her of these murders, too. I couldn't let that happen. There must be some clues in that room. I stealthily slithered out from my hiding place and slipped almost unnoticed behind the captain's legs.

"Paws!" Max shouted at me. "You can't go in there."

She darted under the captain's arm and grabbed for me, but I eluded her.

I'd already spotted something clutched in Berti's outstretched hand, something fluttering in the wind from the open balcony. It was a page ripped from Stella's notepad, the one with the cat riding a polar bear. If the captain saw that, he'd be sure to think Jo had done these awful murders, and maybe with Stella's help.

I grabbed the page in my teeth, ripped it out of Berti's dead hand, and raced toward the open door of the balcony, but Max was too fast for me. She grabbed the note, and tore it out from between my teeth.

"But, Gran!" she exclaimed. She looked at the paper in shocked amazement. "This is a note on your notepaper."

"What?" Stella shoved past the captain. "But I didn't write any note. What does it say?"

"*Meet me in Leroy's suite at 9:00 a.m. sharp,*" Max read. "*Be on time if you want your money.*"

"Give me that note," the captain demanded. "And everyone out of here. This a crime scene."

Max started to hand the note to the captain, but her eyes brightened when she turned it over.

"There's an ink smudge on it," she said. Her voice lit up with excitement. "Maybe a fingerprint."

Jo grabbed the note out of Max's hand.

At this rate everybody's fingerprints would be on it

"But this is evidence," Jo exclaimed. "It'll prove me innocent."

"Don't let her have that," Miriam cried. "She'll destroy it." She tried to snatch the note out of Jo's hands, but the sound of tearing paper filled the room. Both Jo and Miriam stared in disbelief at the fragment of paper held in each of their hands.

"Give those to me," the captain ordered.

Both ladies loosened their grip, and the captain reached

for the torn fragments. Before he could get a grasp on them, a gust of wind snatched them away, wafting them toward the open door.

"Grab them," the captain shouted.

Max jumped for one. I jumped for the other, but it lifted out of my reach and soared toward the balcony. I could clearly see the ink smudge as it whipped through the open door. This was the fragment we needed to find out who the killer was. The wind lifted it and was about to toss it over the railing. I leaped toward it. I would have had it in my paws if the captain hadn't tackled me from behind. He hauled me back onto the balcony.

Stella threw her arms around the both of us nearly knocking us over the railing and out to sea. Tears streamed down her face and plopped into my ears as she squished me between herself and the captain.

"Thank you, thank you, thank you, Gideon," she blubbered. "You saved him again!"

Saved me? The captain hadn't saved me at all. Two seconds more and I'd have had the note. And who'd be the hero then?

I spat a mouthful of salty sea spray onto the captain's fancy shoulder stripes.

CHAPTER 24

"HOUSE ARREST!" JO SPAT out the words as she paced back and forth across Stella's cabin like a caged lion. She still hadn't changed out of her rehearsal gown, and the tattered strands of the skirt slapped against her legs as she paced. I raced after her and tried to catch the flapping tendrils of skirt.

Jo yelped as my claws accidentally scratched across her leg.

"Out of my way, Paws," she ordered. "You want to get stepped on?"

I slid under the bed and continued to watch the swaying strands of skirt as Jo turned and paced back to the window.

"No need to take it out on Paws," Max said, coming to my defence. She sat cross-legged in the corner of the room, repeatedly punching numbers into her cell phone. "It's not his fault we're all under house arrest."

"Well he certainly didn't help, did he?" Jo said. She paced back to the bed and scowled down at the spot where my paws stuck out from under the bed. I pulled them further into my hiding spot. "Barging into the room and grabbing that note," she continued.

"If he hadn't found the note, someone else would have," Max said.

She held her cell phone to her ear, listened a few minutes, and then snapped it shut with disgust.

"Where can Alvin be?" she demanded. She sprang to her feet and joined Jo in pacing to the door. "If it weren't for this house arrest, I'd go out and find the fool. Doesn't he know hiding is making him look guilty?"

"Why don't you both settle down," Stella said.

The bed squeaked and groaned above my head as Stella rolled over and grabbed her purse off the floor. I crouched as low as I could. If Stella and that bed collapsed, I'd be nothing more than a few whiskers sticking out of a grease spot.

"Captain Bonar put us under house arrest for our own safety," Stella continued. "We might as well all get a good night's sleep."

The bed creaked and groaned again, and I squished myself even flatter against the floor. Why couldn't Stella lie still? What was she doing anyway? A tube of lipstick rolled off the bed and onto the floor. Jo strode across to the bed. Her bare foot smacked into the lipstick tube and sent it smashing into my nose. She leaned over the bed.

"Our safety?" she said. She made a disgusted noise with her mouth. "I'm being framed for murder. How safe is that? And you needn't think you'll get off scot free, my friend." She leaned even further over the bed. "That note was printed on your notepaper, Stella. Don't forget that. Someone out there is trying to frame us both, and we're stuck in here unable to do a thing about it."

The bed bounced even more, followed by a scrabbling noise. I slithered out from under it, deciding it would be better to be caught by an angry Jo than squished to a grease spot under the bed.

Stella was kneeling on the bed, the entire contents of her purse spread out before her. She scrabbled through the pile of stuff. Her offensive notepad slid off the bed and landed at my feet. I sniffed at it in disgust. That notepad had gotten us into more trouble than enough.

"What on earth are you doing?" Jo asked.

"I'm looking for my sleeping pills," Stella said. " I know I put a full bottle of them in here before I left, just in case. But they're not here."

I looked accusingly at Max. She'd used them the day she'd tried to put Garvey and Angus Lloyd out of commission so she could see what was in the briefcase. That seemed like weeks ago now so much had happened. Could it really have been only yesterday morning?

"Don't look at me," Max said. "I put them back."

"What on earth were you doing with my sleeping pills?" Stella asked.

"It's a long story, Gran," Max said. She scowled at me as though it were all my fault.

I glared back. No need to take that look with me. I wasn't the one who'd taken the sleeping pills, was I?

"Anyway," Max said. "It's not important."

"Of course it's not important," Jo said. "What's important is figuring out who killed Leroy and who's trying to frame us, and you don't need your sleeping pills for that."

She snatched the notepad off the floor and jumped onto the bed beside Stella.

"Let's go through these notes of yours, put our heads together, and figure it out," Jo said

I groaned. This was going to be a long night. I stretched out full length on the floor and buried my head in my paws.

Who had killed Leroy? I'd been so certain it was the captain. I groaned again at the thought that I now had to strike him off my list. He hadn't killed Tyler and Berti. I knew that for a fact.

And even I had to admit whoever killed Tyler and Berti had been Leroy's murderer as well.

"So who's left on your list?" Jo asked.

"We hadn't gotten around to questioning Miriam Turner," Stella said.

"Nor Patricia," Max added. She jumped onto the bed between Stella and Jo.

"And I don't suppose you asked your darling captain any pertinent questions, either, did you?" Jo said.

Stella bristled. "Really, Jo, I don't know what you've got against the captain. He locked you up because all the evidence pointed to you. What was he supposed to do?"

Jo sniffed. "Maybe he's protecting that son of his," she said.

"Alvin?" Max cried. Her red ponytail slapped Stella in the face as she turned on Jo. "Alvin's no killer."

"Then why's he hiding?" Jo asked.

"He probably saw something," Max admitted. "And the dolt's scared to tell anybody."

"Probably saw his dad do it," Jo muttered half under her breath, but not low enough that Stella hadn't heard.

"Stop it!" Stella ordered. "Captain Bonar didn't kill anyone."

For once I had to reluctantly agree with Stella. I sighed, pushed myself off the floor, and wandered over to my food bowl. With these three caterwauling all night, how was a cat supposed to get any sleep, and without sleep, how was I going to figure out who killed Leroy Garvey? I almost longed for the brig. At least there I was alone. Being under house arrest with these three was more than any cat should have to bear. Not that I'd call it house arrest, exactly. This was no house. This was a ship. Cabin arrest maybe. I crunched as loudly as I could on my kibbles to show my disgust with my noisy roommates, but they paid not the least bit of attention. If only someone had put the three of them under house arrest before they ever embarked on this cruise, none of us would be in this predicament.

"What about Patricia?" Max demanded. Her high-pitched voice grated on my exhausted nerves. I crunched even more loudly. "She's the one that inherits all that money," Max continued. "They say to follow the money, don't they? And I never did believe that sweeter-than-thou attitude of hers."

"This is getting us absolutely nowhere," Stella said.

She was right about that. Now perhaps they'd all settle down and let me get some sleep. How was I going to mull this puzzle over without my valuable catnap. I sat back on my haunches and wiped a few crumbs off my whiskers.

"We can't just go around accusing people without proof," Stella added.

"Then let's go get us some proof," Jo said. She bounced off the bed, shoved her feet into a pair of slippers, and headed for the door. "I'm going to talk to Patricia. Stella, you tackle Miriam Turner, and Max, go find Alvin."

"Find Alvin," Max grumbled "I wish I could. I've already looked everywhere I could think of."

I gave my ears a superior rub. I had a pretty good idea where Alvin was hiding, but I wasn't about to tell these three amateur sleuths. They'd only get him into more trouble.

Max looked at me. "You know where he is, don't you, Paws?" She scooped me up before I could scamper out of reach. "Okay, Aunt Jo, let's go. Paws will lead me to Alvin."

Jo yanked open the door to the cabin and collided with an officer in his stiff white uniform.

"Can I get you anything, Ma'am?" the officer asked.

Jo slammed the door in his face.

"So much for that idea," Stella smirked.

"I know another way out," Max said. Her ponytail flipped defiantly, and she headed for the balcony.

A brisk sea breeze ruffled the hair on the back of my head and sent chills running down my spine. Surely she wasn't going to crawl along the railing. Waves crashed against the side of the ship. I struggled to get free, but Max's grip on me tightened.

"Do be still, Paws," she ordered.

"Here, you better use this," Stella said. She unwound the pink scarf with its floppy strands from around her neck and handed it to Max. "Make a leash for him or he'll run off on you."

The fluffy strands flapped wildly in protest as Max wound the scarf around me in a tight-fitting harness. I hissed my indignation.

"Shush, Paws," Max crooned. "It'll be alright."

Alright? I tried to yowl, but my mouth filled with floppy strands of pink scarf. How could she say it would be alright when she was not only forcing me into criminal activities, but had already fastened a noose about my neck? I sneezed loudly as one of the strands tickled my nose.

"Hush, Paws!" Max ordered. "Do you want someone to hear us?"

What a great idea! Maybe someone would come to my rescue.

I spat out the strands of fluff and opened my mouth to let out a loud yowl, but the yowl froze in my throat as Max clambered onto the railing and grabbed hold of the wall dividing Stella's balcony from the one adjoining it.

I stared down at the turbulent sea far below me. No need to worry about being sent to the brig. We were both going to end up treading water in that icy sea until Davey Jones himself pulled us under and stuck us in his locker.

"Is that safe, Max?" Stella asked.

Great flapping whales' tails! Of course it wasn't safe. I yowled loudly and once more struggled to get free.

"Stay still, Paws!" Max ordered. "Do you want to dump us in the ocean?"

It wasn't me trying to dump us in the ocean. I yowled even more loudly and tried to crawl over her shoulder.

"Maybe this isn't such a good idea, Max," Stella said.

"Nonsense, Gran. It's perfectly safe. I've done it lots of times." Max sidled along the railing and swung one leg around the wall and onto the railing of the balcony next door. "How do you think I've been getting in and out for the last three days without you seeing me? The cabin next door's empty. I've put a piece of tape on the catch of its balcony doors so they don't lock. I get in there and step out the front door with no one any the wiser."

She grinned at Jo and Stella's shocked faces.

"I didn't take five years of gymnastics for nothing," she said.

She maneuvered her right leg around the wall, onto the railing, and then dropped catlike to the balcony of the adjoining cabin. I jumped off her shoulder and tried to get as far away from her as possible, but she tugged me back, tucked me under her arm and headed for the cabin doors.

"Maybe you guys should stay here," Max called over her shoulder. "I'll find Alvin and bring him back. We can question him together."

"Wait!" Stella shouted. "I'm coming too. If you can do it, so can I."

Her spiky-heeled shoes flew over the dividing wall narrowly missing my head. The railing groaned as Stella clambered onto it.

Great balls of fur! Didn't she know scaling balcony dividers was a task for the young and fit? And scaling it in her bare feet wasn't any safer than trying to walk it in high-heeled shoes. She was going to slip.

Even as I yowled another warning, her feet slipped. She shrieked so loudly I was sure someone would hear and come to our rescue, but the sound disappeared in the crashing waves below. Stella clung to the railing, one hand on each side of the divider.

Max lowered me to the balcony floor, raced to the railing, and grabbed Stella's arm.

"I've got you, Gran," she said. "Just throw your leg over the railing."

Stella swung back and forth in an effort to swing her leg high enough to clear the railing. One of her hands slipped. She shrieked. Max's breath came in greater and greater gasps as she struggled to hold onto Stella. I added my weight to Max's, the fluffy pink scarf pulling taut as I dug my claws into the deck. Maybe the two of us could keep the swaying Stella from dropping into the ocean. I had nearly given up hope, certain that any minute now Stella would plunge into the waters below, dragging Max and me with her, when Stella somehow managed to swing her leg over the rail. She thumped onto the deck beside me like a bloated whale.

Jo, as though to prove her superior agility, jumped nimbly down beside us.

I clawed at my make-shift leash, trying desperately to free myself from it. I wasn't going anywhere with these three accidents-waiting-to-happen. But the scarf only wrapped more tightly around my neck.

Max scooped me into her arms, slid the balcony door open and tiptoed into the room. Stella and Jo followed. Max crept quietly across the floor and cautiously opened the door. She looked both ways up and down the hallway, and then set me on the floor in front of her.

"Okay, Paws," she mouthed, being careful not to alert the sleepy guard who leaned against the door to Stella's cabin. "Lead me to Alvin."

CHAPTER 25

I LOOKED TOWARD THE yawning security officer. One yowl out of me would bring him running, and we'd all be back in the cabin safe and sound. Or would we? Knowing Jo, she'd probably karate chop the poor officer, and we'd end up in even worse trouble than before.

I hated to admit it, but maybe Max was right. Maybe it was time to have a chat with Alvin and find out what he knew and why he was hiding. Had he seen something he was afraid to reveal? Or was he in fact the killer? I didn't want him to be the killer, but if he was, he needed to face up to it, not let Jo take the fall for him.

I padded softly down the hallway in the opposite direction to the yawning officer and slipped silently around the corner. Max followed so close on my heels I had to lift up my tail to keep her from treading on it. Stella and Jo stumbled after us, carrying their spiky-heeled stilettos and awkwardly tiptoeing in their bare feet. Once we cleared the corner, they leaned on each other to pull on their spiky heels, and then headed for the elevator, Jo to interrogate Patricia, the fairy princess, and Stella to interrogate Miriam, the siren of doom. I thanked that fickle feline luck that I was with Max and not Stella. I'd rather interrogate Alvin, or even the captain himself, than face the eerie Miriam Turner.

I headed down the stairs to the pool deck and trotted over to the Dolphin Pool and Hot Tubs, almost certain Alvin would be tucked in behind the towel rack. Wasn't there a whisper of guitar music coming from there, or was that just the wind tossing the cart to and fro?

Max must have thought I was headed past the pool to the Sea Nymphs Cafeteria. She jerked on my make-shift leash, pulling me to a choking stop.

"Forget your stomach, Paws," she ordered. Her ponytail flipped angrily. "You're supposed to be leading me to Alvin. Even I know he's not going to be on this deck. It's far too public. He'll be down on the crew deck somewhere."

She tried to drag me back to the staircase, but I dug my claws in and refused to move. She could go traipsing around the crews' quarters if she wanted, but she could do it without me. I knew where Alvin was hiding.

The elevator doors slid open, and I caught a glimpse of the captain's worried face.

Flapping whales' tails. This was no time to be caught by him. I tugged on my leash. Max must have seen the captain, too, because this time she followed as I darted across the deck, skirted the pool, and squeezed through the narrow opening behind the towel rack.

Alvin sat hunched in the corner of the alcove, his ball cap tugged low on his head. He hugged his guitar to him as though clinging to a lifeline. His head popped up as Max squeezed through the opening behind me.

"What are you doing here?" he growled.

"Looking for you, you dolt," Max said. She placed one hand on her hip and glared at him. "Don't you know hiding is making it look like you're the killer?"

A dark shadow blocked what little light had filtered into the alcove. Captain Bonar shoved the towel rack aside and barged into the cubbyhole.

"Is that why you're hiding, son?" the captain asked.

Alvin sprang to his feet and looked accusingly at Max and me.

"You brought my dad," he said, his voice unbelieving.

"Oh, don't blame Max," Captain Bonar said. "She said she didn't know where you were, but I was pretty sure she was lying. I just followed her."

"I wasn't lying," Max said, flicking her ponytail defiantly. "I didn't know where he was. Paws brought me here."

Captain Bonar gave me a salute. "Then I owe you one, Inspector Paws," he said.

I hissed and slid as far away from him as possible. The last thing I'd wanted to do was bring the captain here.

The captain's concerned eyes turned back to Alvin.

"Now listen, son," he said. "If you killed Leroy Garvey and the others, you've got to say so. I'll get you a good lawyer. We'll straighten it out."

Alvin raised his guitar as if about to strike his father with it.

"Are you trying to pin those deaths on me?" he asked. His voice raised to a squeak of disbelief. "How could you? Your own son? You killed them, and you're pinning it on me!"

"What?" Captain Bonar's eyebrows disappeared under this cap. "You think I could kill someone?"

They stared at each other in shock.

Max's excited voice broke the silence. "But if you each thought the other did it, then neither one of you did," she said.

Captain Bonar threw his arms around Alvin and his guitar.

"Oh, son," he said. There were tears in his voice. "I didn't want to believe it, but you just disappeared after Garvey's death. And then when I saw you running away from Tyler and Berti's dead bodies, I knew I had to find you. What were you doing there?"

"I was working," Alvin said. His voice was muffled as he clung to his father. "Decided hiding wasn't a good idea, even if Aunt Miriam thought I should. I was going in to clean Garvey's old cabin. I opened the door to Garvey's old cabin and there they were — Tyler and Berti. I just ran. And then I saw you."

"And you thought I'd killed them. Why would you think that?" the captain asked.

"Aunt Miriam said you'd killed Leroy Garvey. She told me to hide," Alvin said.

"What? When did she tell you this?"

"I was there," Alvin said. "The night Garvey died. I went back. I'd left my guitar case when I stormed out of there. I figured everyone would be gone, and then I saw him lying there on the floor. I grabbed my guitar case and beetled out of there, but I nearly collided with Aunt Miriam. She wanted to know what I was so scared about, and I told her what I'd seen. She said, 'Oh my! Your father ...' and then she told me to hide, to stay away until the investigation was over. She said it would be better for you."

Captain Bonar frowned. "Maybe she thought you'd done it, son, and wanted to keep you safe. No wonder she's so keen to blame it on Jo Bellamy."

My whiskers tingled as the puzzle pieces fell into place. Miriam Turner had indeed been keen to get these murders pinned on Jo, but it wasn't to save her nephew or her brother. She knew perfectly well neither one of them was guilty. She'd killed Garvey herself. Tyler had seen her, and Tyler and Berti were blackmailing her. No wonder she'd insisted on the captain setting Jo free. Miriam had decided to get rid of Berti and Tyler, and she wanted Jo free so Jo would be blamed. Miriam had killed Berti and Tyler using the chair leg Jo had dropped in the hallway. And then she'd had the nerve to show up at the door to Garvey's cabin, her hair still dripping wet from the shower she'd taken to get rid of the evidence of her deed. She'd said she'd been jogging, but she hadn't. She'd killed Tyler and Berti and tried to frame Jo for it. The pieces all fell into place.

Miriam was the killer, and Stella had gone alone to question her. I tugged desperately at my frilly leash and headed for the opening to the pool deck, but Max had dropped my leash. She was already running for the staircase. She must have put the pieces together too. We raced up the stairs together. I only hoped we weren't too late.

CHAPTER 26

THE DOOR TO MIRIAM Turner's cabin was firmly closed. A do-not-disturb sign hung from the handle. I lowered my head and sniffed at the slight opening at the bottom of the door. There was no sound of Stella, but I caught a faint whiff of her perfume. She was either in there or she'd just left. Ignoring the do-not-disturb sign that swung warningly back and forth, I scratched frantically on the door. Max joined me, her fists pounding loudly.

"Mrs. Turner!" Max yelled. "Gran!" She pounded even harder.

The door slid open a crack, and Miriam Turner's disapproving face glared out at us.

"Stop that racket!" she ordered. Her bony finger slid through the crack in the door and tapped at the do-not-disturb sign. "Can't you read? I don't wish to be disturbed," she said. "Now go away."

She tried to close the door, but Max stuck her foot in it to keep it from closing.

"Is Gran here?" Max asked.

"Your grandmother?" Miriam asked. "Now why would you think she'd be here?"

Miriam's foot shifted slightly, and I could see Stella behind her. Stella lay sprawled on the floor, her arms flung wide. An overturned wine glass rolled back and forth beside her, its dregs seeping into the carpet in an ever darkening arc of red.

Were we too late? Was she already dead? I squeezed through the crack in the door, my frilly scarf trailing after me, and rushed toward Stella.

"She is in there," Max shouted. "Get out of the way!" She shoved the door wide open, knocking Miriam Turner against the wall, and rushed in after me.

"Gran! Gran!" Max shouted. "Are you okay?"

She ran toward Stella, but Miriam Turner moved even faster. In one fluid move, she yanked her robe from off the hook on the wall by the bathroom and whipped it around Max's legs, quickly grabbing the end and pulling it tight. Max sprawled on her face, and before she could heave herself upright, Miriam tied the robe tightly around Max's ankles. Max yelled and tried to scramble to her knees, but Miriam, moving with the speed of desperation, grabbed Max's arms and yanked them behind her back. She pulled the belt free from the robe and wrapped it tightly around Max's wrists, tying it in a secure knot.

Max yelled for help.

"Oh, do stop that!" Miriam ordered. "I'm going to have to gag you now."

She looked around her for something to use as a gag and spied the frilly pink scarf around my neck. She tugged it roughly from off my neck and shoulders, and wrapped it tightly around Max's mouth. The fluffy strands of pink wool waved back and forth in the breeze from the open balcony door. Max shook her head back and forth trying to get free of them, and then sneezed loudly.

If she and Stella hadn't been in such danger, I'd have found some enjoyment in the sight of her predicament. Now she knew what it was like to have those fluffy strands tickling her nose.

She rolled onto her back, pulled herself to a sitting position, leaned against the couch, and glared at Miriam Turner.

I too looked at Miriam Turner, but with far more wariness than Max.

It was obvious the siren of doom was not her usual self. She seemed to have lost a little confidence, and was pacing nervously up and down the room. She stopped in front of Max. Her hands shook as she covered her face and peered through her fingers.

"Don't look at me like that," Miriam cried. She rubbed her face with her fingers and resumed her pacing. "Oh why? Why did you come here? Why couldn't you have left well enough alone? You and your meddling grandmother."

Max awkwardly pointed her head towards Stella and mumbled something through the scarf. It sounded like, "Is she dead?"

I leaned over Stella's body and licked her nose. A faint breath escaped her nostrils. She was still breathing. Her eyes flickered open and then drooped shut again. I breathed a sigh of relief. She wasn't dead, just sleeping, but it was an awfully deep sleep. Her wine must have had some sort of sedative in it, but who knows how much. I needed to wake her up. I licked frantically at her face.

"I'm so glad you brought the cat with you, though," Miriam Turner said.

I looked warily over my shoulder. Being wanted by Miriam Turner was not a welcoming thought, and the scheming look in her eye was even more unnerving. I was halfway across the room by the time she lunged for me. I raced into the bathroom and jumped onto the counter. From here I'd be able to fend her off.

But Miriam didn't chase after me. Instead she returned

to her pacing. She was hugging herself tightly now, her hands rubbing up and down her arms. Another shiver of fear trembled up my spine. The old Miriam Turner was scary enough. This new, obviously nervous and frightened version of her, was beyond scary.

Miriam looked in at me as she paced past the door.

"Doesn't matter," she muttered, as though talking to herself. "He can't get out. I'll get him later. I have to think. I have to think."

I too had to think. I lowered myself to a crouch on the countertop and rested my head on my paws. The cool of the marble eased my panic. There must be something I could do. I looked around for ideas, and my eye caught sight of the vial beside me. That looked like Stella's missing bottle of sleeping pills. I sat up and reached for the bottle. I could see bits of crushed pill in the sink. Miriam must have laced Stella's wine with sleeping pills, and a lot of them by the looks of it. The bottle was nearly empty.

I knocked the vial off the counter and jumped down after it. Batting it back and forth with my paws, I chased it into the other room and rolled it over to Max.

"You stole Gran's sleeping pills," Max mumbled through the scarf. Her eyes glared accusingly at Miriam.

Miriam stopped pacing and wheeled around to face Max.

"I didn't steal them," she snapped. "That grandmother of yours was forever dropping things."

I remembered Stella dropping her purse as she came in to the rehearsal dinner. Miriam Turner had picked up Stella's notepad and returned it to her with a sarcastic comment. Had she picked up Stella's sleeping pills then, too?

"I merely confiscated those pills for your grandmother's own good," Miriam continued. "I don't believe in sleeping pills.

A little discipline and self control is all a person needs for a good night's sleep."

Max mumbled something unintelligible, nodded towards Stella, and then scowled accusingly at Miriam.

Miriam looked at Stella's prone body. She hugged herself tightly again and started rubbing her arms.

"Well, I wouldn't have given them to her if she hadn't come here nosing around, would I?" she said defensively. "Oh why did she have to meddle? Why couldn't she leave well enough alone? I didn't mean for this to happen." She rubbed her face with her hands as though to rub the nightmare away.

"I didn't mean for any of it to happen," she said. "I saw your Aunt Jo's scarf waving there on the railing. If only I'd left it there. But it was an expensive scarf. So careless of Jo. She was always careless, just like your grandmother."

She looked over at Stella again, and then quickly away.

"I don't know why I took it into Neptune's Loft. Why didn't I just hang on to it and give it back to Jo?"

She shook her head and resumed pacing, striding back and forth across the room, rubbing her arms.

I scurried under the bed to keep out of her way.

"I guess I just wanted to have a look at Garvey. See him in pain," she said. "See him suffering the way he'd made me and Clyde suffer."

She stopped in front of Max, and hugged herself even tighter.

"Don't look at me with those accusing eyes," she said. "I didn't intend to kill him. He invited me in. Said he had something to discuss with me. I was pretty sure he wanted to talk about my dealings with his daughter. I have to admit I was looking forward to rubbing it in that Patricia was beginning to see him for who he really was. He poured me a glass of scotch, slid it across the table, and then told me he didn't like the way

I'd been influencing his daughter and it had to stop. I told him his daughter was over eighteen and capable of making her own decisions."

The bed spring pressed against my ears as Miriam sank onto the bed above me. Had the weight of her actions become too heavy for her to carry around the room?

I squirmed out from under the bed and padded over to Stella. She was still deep in sleep. If only I could wake her. I started once more licking her face, her eyes, her nose, her chin, while Miriam continued her confession.

"Garvey smiled at me — that unpleasant, gloating smile of his — and then he slid his glasses off with his left hand, tapped them annoyingly against that gaudy ring of his, and proceeded to inform me that it would be in my best interests to have nothing further to do with his daughter. I laughed in his face. Told him he couldn't control the whole world, and he had no hold over me. I wasn't one of his employees. He simply smiled and flipped the laptop around so I could read it. It was a draft email to Evelyn Pryor, the head of my department. And as if the words in front of my eyes weren't enough, he started quoting it to me.

"*My dear Evelyn, I'm writing to you on a rather delicate matter involving one of your staff, a certain Miriam Turner, who happens to be one of my fellow passengers on a cruise to Alaska. She took quite an avid interest in my daughter, Patricia. You can imagine both my daughter's and my distress when Mrs. Turner made what can only be described as immoral advances toward my daughter. In order to protect my daughter from further distress, I prefer not to issue formal charges, but I do want to ask you, both as a friend and a concerned citizen, to immediately dismiss Mrs. Turner from your employ to protect the other young women under her influence.*

"I picked up the nearest heavy object, threw it at his head, grabbed the laptop, and ran out of the room."

Miriam suddenly clapped her hands together, as though she'd just found the answer to some tricky problem. She bounced to her feet.

"It was all meant to be, don't you see?" she asked Max, her excitement growing. "It was fate. He was an evil man, and fate wanted him dead. Only fate could have broken off that shard of ice and had it pierce through his eye. He was meant to die, and I was just the chosen instrument. I did the world a favor getting rid of him."

"What about Tyler?" Max mumbled accusingly.

"That was unfortunate, of course" Miriam said, her voice once more confident and clipped. "Tyler was on the deck outside the window. He saw it all. And that greedy mother of his pushed him into blackmailing me. I had no choice, did I? It was either them or me, and in all fairness, who would you say contributes more to this world? Do you know how many young women I've been able to help?"

Max mumbled something through the scarf. It sounded more like a snort, than any intelligible expression. I could see she was rubbing her wrists against the bottom of the couch, trying to loosen the knot, but Miriam didn't seem to notice.

"At least I had time to plan properly for Tyler and Berti's departure," Miriam said. A smile of self congratulation flitted across her face. "Jo was already being blamed for Garvey's murder. It only made sense to frame her for these ones. It was a stroke of genius typing the note on your grandmother's notepaper. I'd taken that page for quite another purpose. Thought I'd use it to put a wedge between Gideon and her. He was just getting way too attached to her for his own good. But this seemed an even better use for it. Then I persuaded Gideon to let Jo out for a while, and Jo played right into my hands. She insisted on getting away from me, which gave me all the time I needed to do the job, shower, and return to the scene of the crime, where of course I bewailed the fact it was all my fault and that I should never have persuaded Gideon to let Jo go free."

"Why Gran? Why me?" Max mumbled.

Miriam frowned.

"If only you hadn't meddled," Miriam scolded. "Your grandmother figured it out, you see, when she saw the sani-wipe in my hand. I'd just poured myself a glass of wine when she barged in here, and I was wiping it clean before drinking from it. I never drink from a glass without wiping it clean. One can pick up so many germs that way. Your grandmother said they'd wondered why there were no fingerprints at all on the extra glass of scotch. And then she laughed. 'Of course,' she said. 'It had to be you. Who else would retrieve Jo's scarf?'"

Miriam sighed and looked sadly at Max.

"I'm sorry about you, though, Max. Truly, I am," she said. "But you see, don't you, that I can't let you go? Not now that you've seen your grandmother like that."

"They won't blame Aunt Jo for Gran and my murders," Max mumbled. "You won't get away with it."

"But of course they won't blame your Aunt Jo," Miriam said. She looked straight at me, and I felt the fur on the back of my neck rise. "They'll blame the cat."

She lunged for me, but I was quicker. I jumped into Stella's large tote bag that leaned conveniently against the end of the couch.

Miriam laughed, a cold, brittle laugh that increased the shivers of fear racing up and down my spine.

"Never mind," she said. "That's as good a place as any for him. He's going overboard, you see."

Overboard? She'd been threatening that from the day I set foot on this ship.

"And everyone knows your grandmother is crazy enough to jump in after him, or topple over the railing trying to reach him. And we know you'd do anything to try to save your grandmother."

Cat-o-Nine-Tails! Miriam's plan might indeed work if I didn't do something quickly. But what could I do? I sank lower into the tote bag.

Something cold and hard pressed against my stomach. Stella's tape recorder. Had she had time to turn it on? I squirmed around to get a better look at it. The record light blinked reassuringly. Good for Stella. Now all I needed to do was get this tape recorder to someone right away before Miriam could implement her plan. So how was I going to do that with the door firmly shut? The only way out was to crawl along the railing. My whiskers trembled at the very thought. It had been hard enough with Max clutching onto me. Weighted down with a cumbersome tape recorder, I'd be facing almost certain death.

"No more time for talk," Miriam said. Her voice took on the authority of a drill master. "Time to put this plan in action."

It was now or never. I grabbed the handle of the tape recorder in my mouth, jumped out of the tote bag, and raced through the open door to the balcony.

Miriam jumped off the bed and raced after me. "Stop!" she yelled.

I leaped onto the railing. The recorder thumped against the plexi-glass below me. I tried to pull it up further, but my back feet slipped. I clung to the railing, my back feet dangling. Below me I could hear the pounding waves. In front of me I could see Miriam Turner, the siren of doom, her eyes flashing with anger, her mouth open in a scream of rage.

She lunged toward the open door and me, but Max's tethered feet swung upward catching Miriam in the shin. Miriam stumbled and sprawled headlong right on top of Stella. Stella groaned, pried open one eyelid, and then let if fall shut again.

I tried to yowl for her to wake up, tell her Max needed her help, but with the strap of the recorder stuffed in my mouth, my yowl was no more than a weak mew that easily carried off in the breeze.

Miriam struggled to get to her feet, but Max launched herself in the air and landed full length on top of Miriam, once more knocking her face down on top of Stella. Stella grunted. Her eyelids once more fluttered, and then her arm flopped across Miriam's head, pinning Miriam to her chest. Miriam kicked and struggled, but she was firmly sandwiched between Stella and Max.

Max lifted her head. Her frantic eyes stared into mine.

"Go!" she mumbled through her scarf. "Get help! Get the captain!"

CHAPTER 27

THE CAPTAIN? JUST THE thought of dragging that widow-hunting Don Juan in to rescue Stella was enough to make my whiskers twinge. If he came to the rescue, Stella would be swooning at his feet. But who else could get into Miriam's cabin easily and quickly? And it's true the captain seemed to be the only one on this whole ship who understood my sign language. Not that it did much good. He rarely listened to what I said or did what I wanted. But I had to admit the captain was the best chance at rescuing Stella and Max.

I swallowed my distaste for dragging the captain to the rescue, along with my fear of the angry waters below me, and pulled myself slowly upward until my body sprawled lengthwise along the railing. I cautiously slithered forward. The tape recorder bumped against the plexi-glass partition below, it's weight trying to derail me. I thought about letting it drop to the deck — I'd be able to move much more quickly that way — but without the tape recorder, chances were the captain wouldn't follow me to Miriam's cabin. He'd simply toss me into the brig and then what would happen to Stella and Max?

I struggled on, and barely dared to breathe as I slithered around the partition, dropped to the deck below, and tried to get my bearings. I was relieved to see it wasn't another balcony, but the landing beside the stairwell. Using a strength I didn't know I'd possessed, I swung the tape recorder around the partition and dragged it down beside me.

Finding the captain was my next problem. Would he and Alvin still be in the hidey hole behind the towel rack? Chances were low, but I decided to try that first. I dragged the tape recorder up the stairs to the pool deck.

I heard their voices long before I'd reached the top of the stairs. The captain's voice was quieter than usual and more controlled. Alvin's was high-pitched and seething with anger.

"Look, son," the captain said. "I know I've made mistakes."

Alvin snorted. "You think?" he asked. The question hung with sarcasm.

"I'm sorry," the captain said. "I wish I'd done things differently. I was wrong."

I stopped in my tracks. The captain admitting he was wrong? That was a first. Even Alvin was silent.

"What can I do to make this right?" the captain asked. "I don't want to lose you. You're my son. I love you."

I dragged the tape recorder up the last step of the stairs. I could see them now. They were no longer tucked in behind the towel rack, but sitting on the floor leaning against it. Alvin jumped to his feet and towered angrily over his father.

"Love me?" Alvin shouted. "Then why did you lie to me about my mother?"

"I didn't lie to you," the captain said. "I told you she was dead. I just didn't tell you how she died."

"And you didn't tell me she was a musician," Alvin accused.

The captain didn't reply, merely lowered his head and ran a hand through his hair.

"Don't you get it, Dad?" Alvin asked. He lowered his voice and looked pleadingly at his father. "It's in my blood. Music is in my blood. It's not even a choice for me. I have to play."

The captain rose to his feet and put a hand on Alvin's shoulder.

"Don't you get it, Alvin?" he asked softly. "I don't want the same thing to happen to you that happened to your mother."

Were those real tears in his eyes? I scurried over to them. The reluctant tape recorder bumped along behind me. I hated to interrupt this tender scene, but Stella and Max were in danger.

Alvin at least was relieved to see me. His father's tears seemed to make him a little uncomfortable.

"Look, Dad! It's Inspector Paws!" he exclaimed.

He tried to pull away from his father's hand, but the captain's grip on his arm tightened. He bent his knees slightly, scooped me up, clutched me close to his side, and continued his conversation as though I didn't exist.

"Look, son," he said. "Couldn't you give it just one more year? Take a business course, learn a trade, something to fall back on?"

Cat-o-Nine-Tails! They could have this argument later. Stella and Max needed help right now. I struggled to free myself. The tape recorder banged against the captain's leg, but he simply ignored it. I opened my mouth and yowled loudly. The tape recorder crashed to the deck.

"What's he doing with a tape recorder?" Alvin asked. He scooped it up from the deck. "And where's Max? He left with Max."

Alvin quickly rewound the tape recorder and pressed play. Miriam's eerie voice drifted out of the box.

"He's going overboard, you see. And everyone knows Stella is crazy enough to jump in after him, or topple over the railing trying to reach him. And we know you'd do anything to try to save your grandmother."

"That's Aunt Miriam!" Alvin exclaimed. "And she's got Max."

He shoved past his father and raced for the stairwell.

Captain Bonar dropped me to the deck like he was discarding a dirty shirt, and raced after Alvin, but not before he knocked the rack of towels over. They tumbled on top of me, blocking out the light.

I tunneled my way out from under the mountain of towels, bounded down the stairs three at a time, and raced down the hallway to Miriam's door, but I was too late. The door slammed in my face.

I sprawled on the floor with my nose pressed to the crack below the door. I could hear scuffling noises, Miriam's cry of alarm, and then a chilling silence. Finally, the captain's worried voice seeped through the crack.

"Stella, are you okay?" he asked.

Stella didn't reply. Had we gotten here too late? I scratched frantically on the door, but they paid no attention to me.

"About time you got here," Max said from inside the room. Her voice had returned to normal so they must have removed the fluffy scarf.

And then I heard Stella's groggy voice drift under the door. She was alive. I breathed a sigh of relief, but my relief soon turned to dismay.

"Oh, Gideon," Stella murmured. "I just knew you'd rescue me. My knight in shining armor."

Great hairy fur balls! She was swooning at his feet. I scratched angrily at the door, but they continued to ignore me. I slumped to the floor and licked angrily at my side. What a pair of traitors! I should have let the pair of them drown if that's all the thanks they could give me.

CHAPTER 28

"Isn't Captain Bonar wonderful?" Stella gushed. She buried her nose in the huge bouquet of flowers he'd sent her.

Jo and Max made matching gagging sounds. I wanted to gag too, but gagging would have given away my hiding spot. I burrowed deeper under the scarf in the bottom of Stella's straw tote bag and peered through the mesh.

"Really, Stella," Jo said. "If you've finished gushing over your heroic captain and drooling over those stinking flowers he sent you, we could use a hand looking for that dratted cat of yours. We're supposed to be disembarking already."

She dropped to her knees and peered under the bed. Max opened the closet doors, pulled out the life jackets, and even checked the droopy laundry bag, although it was quite obvious there was no cat hanging inside it. Humans! They had so little sense.

I stretched full length and licked at my paws. Stella's jar of hand cream rolled across my back. Her notepad slid sideways, and the pen jabbed into my ribs. The tote bag teetered precariously on the edge of the night table, and then stood still. I froze in place and peered through the mesh. Nobody had noticed the jiggling tote bag. I breathed a sigh of relief. Much too soon to reveal my whereabouts. They hadn't suffered enough yet. I watched them scurry around the cabin searching every crack and cranny. Stella opened the balcony door.

"Inspector Paws!" she called.

As though I'd be hiding out there. I'd had more than enough of balconies that hung above that dreadful sea.

"Inspector Paws!" Stella called again, her voice laced with an edge of panic.

About time she showed some concern for me. It had been two days since the rescue, and she hadn't even bothered to thank me for my part in it. She'd been too busy worshiping the mighty Captain Bonar, her knight in shining armor. Even when she was getting her stomach pumped, she was singing his praises, as though he'd walked into Miriam's cabin single-handedly and carried Stella to safety. He hadn't even lifted her. The paramedics had undertaken that mammoth task, and nearly ran right over me in the process. I had bruises on my tail to show for it.

And Max? I watched her open the door and peer up and down the hallway. Max had been so busy chasing around the boat after Alvin, taking in all the last minute pleasures the boat had to offer, she barely acknowledged me. Until this morning.

This morning she'd had the audacity to pull me out of a much-needed catnap, squish the living daylights out of me, and moan, "Oh, Inspector Paws, don't you wish this cruise could last forever?"

I scrabbled out of her clutches and jumped into the nearest hiding place I could find —Stella's gigantic tote bag.

"Well he's not in this cabin. We've looked everywhere," Jo said. She crammed the last pair of Stella's shoes back into the shoe bag, which she'd dumped out on the cabin floor.

"Then we'd better search the rest of the ship. He must have

gotten out," Max said. She headed for the door with Jo on her heels, but Stella hung back.

"You two go," Stella said. "Captain Bonar asked me to wait here for him. Said he had something to discuss."

Jo and Max made further gagging sounds and then disappeared into the hallway.

I almost followed them. The last thing I wanted was to witness another mushy meeting between Stella and the captain, but witness it I did.

No sooner had the captain tapped on the door, than Stella flung it open, and hurled herself into his arms. I felt the growl build inside me. How dare she throw herself at the captain like that? She belonged to Ernie. Ernie was the only one allowed to hold her like that and murmur in her ear like that, and really, why did the human variety find sucking on each others' mouths so exciting?

I closed my eyes, and tried not to watch, but I couldn't keep them closed. Someone had to keep an eye on the two of them.

"Oh, Gideon," Stella said, breaking away from his clutches. "We've got to find Paws. He's gone missing again."

The captain took her hand and pulled her toward the balcony.

"Never mind the cat, Stella," he said. "He'll show up. Probably snuck off to the cafeteria, raiding the last of the tuna. Come on out here," he continued. "I've got something to show you."

His smile reminded me of the time I'd swallowed a whole chunk of cheese before Stella could steal it back. What was he up to?

I scrambled out of the tote bag and followed after them.

They were so busy gazing into each other's eyes, they didn't notice me slip through the balcony door and slide under the lounge chair.

The captain pulled a small box out of his pocket. That looked like a jeweler's box. He opened it and pulled out a diamond ring that sparkled in the sunlight. He tucked the box back into his pocket and dropped to one knee in front of Stella.

Flapping whales' tails! He was going to ask her to marry him. What if she said yes? What if we had to live on this boat forever?

I looked up at Stella's face. Her eyes sparkled brighter than the diamond in the ring.

An even worse thought crossed my mind. What if Stella invited him into Ernie's house? What if he took over Ernie's study, Ernie's chair by the fire?

"Stella Clayton," the captain said. His voice was a little husky. "Since you insist on chasing danger, I think you need a fulltime bodyguard, one that loves you to distraction." He smiled up at her. "I'd like to apply for the job," he said. He held the ring up towards her. "Will you marry me?"

No! I yowled. I had to stop this. I leaped out from under the table, lunged for the ring, and batted it out of his fingers. It clinked onto the deck. I swatted it toward the railing and watched it slide through the crack below the glass and drop down into the briny blue, a gift for Davey Jones' locker.

I patted myself on the back, and turned back to look at Stella. There'd be no wedding.

But my self-congratulation came too soon. Apparently the ring didn't matter.

Stella pulled the captain to his feet, threw her arms around him, and danced in circles.

"Yes! Yes! Yes!" she shouted.

No! No! No! I yowled, but only one lone seagull heard my wail.

Printed in the United States
By Bookmasters